Dedalus European Classics
General Editor: Timothy Lane

THE SOLDIER'S HAT

(AND OTHER STORIES)

Sidonie-Gabrielle Colette

THE SOLDIER'S HAT

(AND OTHER STORIES)

translated
with an introduction & notes by
Graham Anderson

Dedalus

Published in the UK by Dedalus Limited
24-26, St Judith's Lane, Sawtry, Cambs, PE28 5XE
info@dedalusbooks.com
www.dedalusbooks.com

ISBN printed book 978 1 915568 61 8
ISBN ebook 978 1 915568 70 0

Dedalus is distributed in the USA & Canada by SCB Distributors
15608 South New Century Drive, Gardena, CA 90248
info@scbdistributors.com www.scbdistributors.com

Dedalus is distributed in Australia by Peribo Pty Ltd
58, Beaumont Road, Mount Kuring-gai, N.S.W. 2080
info@peribo.com.au www.peribo.com.au

First published in France in 1943
First published by Dedalus in 2025

Printed and bound in the UK by Clays Elcograf S.p.A.
Typeset by Marie Lane

A C.I.P. listing for this book is available on request.

The Author

Sidonie-Gabrielle Colette was born in rural Burgundy in 1873. At twenty, she married Henry Gauthier-Villars, known as "Willy", a critic, journalist and self-promoting man of letters, fourteen years older than herself. Soon immersed in his Parisian literary world, she wrote for him the sensational and highly successful *Claudine* series of novels. But the pair separated in 1906 and were divorced in 1910. She subsequently married twice more. Her writing career continued in spite of much turmoil, including spells as a dancer, mime artist and actor. Among her most renowned works are *La vagabonde* (1910), *Chéri* (1920), *Le blé en herbe* (1923), *La naissance du jour* (1928) and *Gigi* (1944).

Her literary fame was matched by admiration for her strong-minded, independent and often controversial lifestyle. Although crippled by arthritis in her last decade, she nevertheless remained active throughout the war years in Nazi-occupied Paris, having become by now the *grande dame* of French literature. She was elected president of the Académie Goncourt in 1949 and appointed Grand Officier in the Légion d'honneur in 1953. On her death in August 1954, she became the first woman in France to be honoured by a state funeral.

The Translator

Graham Anderson was born in London. After reading French and Italian at Cambridge, he worked on the book pages of *City Limits* and reviewed fiction for *The Independent* and *The Sunday Telegraph*. As a translator, he has developed versions of French plays, both classic and contemporary for the NT and the Gate Theatre, with performances both here and in the USA.

His translations for Dedalus from French are *Sappho* by Alphonse Daudet, *Chasing the Dream* and *A Woman's Affair* by Liane de Pougy, *This was the Man* (*Lui*) by Louise Colet, *This Woman, This Man* (*Elle et Lui*) by George Sand, *The Innocent Libertine* and *The Soldier's Hat* (*and other stories*) by Colette.

His own short fiction has won or been shortlisted for three literary prizes. He is married and lives in Oxfordshire.

INTRODUCTION

By March 1943, when *Le képi* (*The Soldier's Hat*) was published, Colette had just turned seventy; her mobility was becoming increasingly impaired by arthritis; and to make her confinement all the more painful, Paris was under Nazi occupation.

The slim young woman of the early 1900s was now fat; the long, plaited rope of hair had turned into a wiry, henna-tinted crop; but the small pointed face and the penetrating blue eyes still announced a writer with all her faculties.

In the thirty or more years since reclaiming her rights to the two *Minne* novellas which would become, in 1909 and under her own name, the novel *L'ingénue libertine* (*The Innocent Libertine*), Colette had produced a huge body of work, including amongst some thirty works of fiction *La vagabonde*, the celebrated *Chéri*, *Le blé en herbe*, *La fin de chéri*, *La naissance du jour*, *Duo* and *La chatte*.

Following her eventual divorce from Willy—Henry Gauthier-Villars, her Svengali-like mentor and tormentor—she had married twice more. Her second husband, Henry de Jouvenel (1876-1935), a diplomat and journalist, had been the editor of Colette's articles for the newspaper *Le Matin*. They married in 1912, and a daughter, Colette de Jouvenel, was born in 1913, when Colette was forty. Henry de Jouvenel's son by his first marriage, Bertrand, born in 1903, began an affair with his stepmother when still a teenager in 1920. The relationship caused a scandal which led to Colette's second divorce in 1924, but was also the inspiration behind her novel of 1923, *Le blé en herbe* (*The Ripening Seed*).

In 1925, Colette was introduced at a friend's house to Maurice Goudeket, a handsome but reserved man, Jewish, with a French mother and a Dutch father, who worked as a dealer in pearls and had ambitions as a writer. He was 35, she 52. They were lovers for ten years before marrying in 1935, an event occasioned by their being sent by the papers for which they were then writing, *La République* (Colette) and *France Soir* (Goudeket) to travel to New York on the maiden voyage of the transatlantic liner *Normandie*. Maurice Goudeket had half-jokingly remarked that they would not be allowed to share a room in any American hotel, unless, of course, they were to marry. (1) The swiftly arranged and sparsely attended civil ceremony initiated the third and most serene of Colette's marriages. Goudeket was to prove a lifelong support to her both as protector and promoter of her literary reputation and as carer in her embattled old age.

The *Normandie*, incidentally, was to have a brief career.

With war threatening, the ship took refuge in New York harbour when hostilities became seemingly unavoidable. There, it was interned by the US government on 3rd September 1939. Trapped for two years, the vessel was, after America's entry into the war, transferred to the US Navy. Whilst undergoing conversion to a troop ship, it caught fire, in February 1942, and capsized. The luckless former holder of the Blue Riband was eventually sent for scrapping in 1946.

The looming war had never made a great distraction from their work for Colette and Maurice. Like Jane Austen with the Napoleonic Wars, Colette's writing never made any allusion to the politics of the day (not that the unlikely pairing of Austen and Colette can be made in many other respects). When war came, Colette was writing, amongst other things, articles on beauty for the women's magazine *Marie-Claire*, whilst simultaneously suffering painful problems with her hips and teeth. She and Maurice fled Paris at the approach of the Germans in May 1940, but after many temporary moves, returned to their apartment in the *Palais Royal* in September. A volume of novellas, *Chambre d'hôtel* (*Chance Acquaintances*), was published by Fayard in December. It was in this same month, that having felt twinges of discomfort in her legs for the past year, Colette submitted to an X-ray, which showed she had rheumatoid arthritis in both hips. By the winter of 1940-41, the German occupiers had seized control of most of France's newspapers, installing editors sympathetic to their cause. Censorship had come in. In spite of the distaste it inspired, Colette continued to contribute (non-political) articles to a number of papers and magazines under new, Nazi-approved editorship: *Le Petit Parisien*, a popular daily; *Gringoire*, a right-wing political and literary weekly which switched from its anti-war stance of the late 1930s to becoming a supporter of the Vichy government after the defeat of France; and *La Gerbe*, a pro-Nazi weekly.

Like most of the French population, especially those in occupied Paris, Colette felt there was nothing she could actively do, and she still had her living to make. She had recognised in herself a certain passivity, (2), a tendency to allow the outside world to be what it would, while her inner life and her work continued within their narrower horizons. All this changed when Maurice Goudeket was arrested by the Gestapo in a sweep intended to round up prominent Jewish Parisians. While Maurice was removed from their apartment, calmly enough and with bag packed, Colette began a frantic campaign to have him freed. The prisoners were held in a detention camp in Compiègne, where the conditions were spartan but not hostile. After seven weeks of agitated comings and goings, Colette succeeded in obtaining Maurice's release, at the prompting it seems of the French wife of the German ambassador. The few months of calm that followed were once again disturbed when the German command issued directions that French Jews would be obliged to wear a yellow star. And not long after, in July of 1942, there began the mass deportation of French Jews to the concentration camps. Feeling his continued presence was a danger to them both, Maurice escaped to friends in Saint-Tropez, in the free zone, where he stayed for several months. At the end of the year the Germans responded to the Allied landings in North Africa by moving into and taking control of the so-called 'free France' of the Vichy government, and Maurice was forced to flee again. This time, after some perilous moments, he returned to Paris, where for the next eighteen months he avoided the danger of another pre-dawn raid by absenting himself at night-time to a servant's quarters and emerging only after nine in the morning. (3) Whether this ruse was sophisticated enough to work, or whether he was simply lucky, there was no further trouble before Paris was liberated in August 1944.

Throughout all these difficult times, Colette continued to work. Her physical incapacity was becoming increasingly burdensome—she bought herself a motorised wheelchair in June 1942—but she would go on to write some of her most compelling stories and novellas. She had already published her only novel of the war years (and her last), *Julie de Carneilhan*, in December 1941. It has come under question for its unsympathetic portrayal of what is taken to be Henry de Jouvenel, and of the riches of his first and (after Colette) third wives, both of them Jewish. The novel was admired by many and despised by some. In the France of Alfred Dreyfus, the ugly face of antisemitism was barely concealed at all; under the Nazi occupation of 1940, sympathisers willingly raised it again. For Colette, as perhaps for large sections of the population, antisemitism was not so much active, or insistent, but as Colette's friend Renée Hamon once remarked, "native". (4)

*

Despite the personal difficulties of its author and the pressures of sustaining a career in wartime, *Le képi*, a collection of two novellas and two short stories, is the book that contains the best of Colette's notably more relaxed and pure fiction in these later years. In it, she exhibits, more than in any other similar volume, a wide variety of techniques, an easy beauty and directness of language, and a rare empathy for the innocent foolishness of people in love.

The title story relates, in glimpses, the late-flowering love affair of a middle-aged friend of the narrator. Marco—her meaningless pen-name reflects her obscurity as a ghost writer—toils to earn a living as a purveyor of cheap sensational literature for newspaper serialisation. A jokey response to a lonely-hearts advertisement leads to the sudden blaze of an unexpected affair, for which the twenty-five-year-old Colette becomes her mentor. In the background, the men in Colette's life—these are real people, Willy, her husband at the time, and Paul Masson, her friend—fire off cynical and misogynistic remarks. The incident that dooms this affair is full of pathos. All this is seen through the prism of the narrator's own busy and complicated life, a device both distancing and intimate.

Le tendron (*The Budding Shoot*), has the more classical and straightforward device of the protagonist, Albin Chaveriat, telling his story uninterrupted to his hostess, our narrator. Here, the voice is entirely that of Chaveriat, a man of advanced years recounting the adventure which cured him, long ago, of his predilection for young girls. The tone is dignified and humorous, a confession not so much remorseful as wry. We are drawn, if not to condone, then to sympathise with behaviour which would be scandalous, and possibly criminal today, but which would, a century ago, have been considered merely unwise. Even at the time though, Colette would have been aware she was treading on thin ice. It is her lightness of touch, her vivid rendering of the country setting, that invest the story with its peculiar charm.

La cire verte (*The Green Sealing Wax*) is another retreat into the past. As in many of Colette's later writings, there is a nostalgic flavour to the whole volume, the action of whose stories takes place at four different periods between 1888 and 1923. This time, Colette is a fifteen-year-old in her native Burgundy village of Saint-Sauveur-en-Puisaye. The story is as much concerned with the flavour and the personalities of her early life as with the incident relating to the green sealing wax, which occupies only a small, though pungent, part of the story. The skill with which the two are linked gives the story its extra kick and reveals a Colette still very much a master of her trade, especially when one remembers the upheavals of the year it was written, 1942.

Armande is that most uncommon of things in the Colette catalogue, a gentle and kindly tale of true love rescued from the failings of human misunderstanding. It is not without its sharper moments, in the character of Maxime's sister and in Maxime's own duplicity at the crucial moment. And *Armande* raises none of the questions about autobiographical authenticity that surround many of her writings in which a real or fictionalised Colette plays a part. It rounds off this short collection with a flourish, as if to prove Colette a more temperate, generous writer than some critics had supposed.

*

Le képi was published in March 1943. The next year saw another collection, headed by *Gigi*, one of her most famous novellas. It was accompanied by two short stories, *Noces* and

Flora et Pomona, and a longer story, *La dame du photographe*. This volume was first published in Lausanne by the *Guilde du livre*. Ferenczi republished it a year later, with *Noces* removed and *L'Enfant malade,* the last fiction Colette wrote, in its place.

As an appendix to *Le képi*, this present volume also includes the "lost" story *Noces* (*A Wedding*). It is here because it shows Colette midway between the fifteen-year-old of The Green Sealing Wax and the twenty-five-year-old of The Soldier's Hat. The first is set in Colette's home village of Saint-Sauveur-en-Puisaye, in northern Burgundy, the second in two different Parisian apartments from which her husband Willy's literary operations were carried out. *Noces*, as its title suggests, is the key moment linking these two worlds, taking Colette on the first steps of the journey that would see her far outdistance her husband. It provides compelling insights into the brash, punning, satirical journalism that ran alongside Willy's more serious work as a music critic. It shows also, the degree to which he leant on others' ideas and contributions, in the unlikely shape of Colette's brother Achille in this case.

More significant is the atmosphere of this story. Although it is scattered with typical asides and humorous observations, the prevailing tone is undoubtably bleak. Colette seems to be sleepwalking into a marriage she is only half prepared for. The mixture of passive acceptance and assertive independence is a feature of much of Colette's life story, and in *Noces* the resulting sense of dislocation is particularly strong. The very elements she chooses to include, in a story called "A Wedding", are odd. We witness no actual wedding but are caught with Colette in the limbo-like aftermath of the ceremony, when half the small party of guests have gone off drinking in a village bar and others are playing word games at the table. Colette meanwhile, is in the garden alone.

The wedding took place in fact, not in Saint-Sauveur, but in Châtillon-sur-Loing, some forty kilometres away. The Colette family had been forced to sell the house in Saint-Sauveur in 1891 following the collapse of the family finances. And of the family members, it is notable that only Sido, Colette's mother, is given her name. Most telling of all, Henry Gauthier-Villars, Willy, is referred to only as "my fiancé" or "my husband".

Colette's vivid recollection, at the age of seventy, in 1943, of the sense of alienation she felt on what was to prove perhaps the key day of her future career, makes *Noces*, a story packed with evocative details of her past life and indications of the life to come, well worth rediscovering.

After *Le képi* and the two versions of *Gigi*, Colette went on to publish three further books, of memoirs and reminiscences: *Paris de ma fenêtre* (*Paris from my Window*, 1944), *L'Etoile vesper* (*The Evening Star*, 1946) and *Le fanal bleu* (*The Blue Lamp*, 1949). Apart from letters to friends, she wrote nothing more. She lived on, severely crippled, devotedly attended by Maurice and by her long-time personal maid Pauline, for another five years. Elected to the *Académie Goncourt* in 1945, she became its president in 1949, and in 1953 was appointed *Grand Officier* in the *Légion d'honneur*. She died on 3rd August 1954. Although denied a church funeral as a consequence of her two divorces, she was nevertheless awarded a state funeral, the first woman in France to be so honoured.

*

In conjunction with *The Soldier's Hat*, Dedalus publishes *The Innocent Libertine* (*L'ingénue libertine*), the earliest writings to be rescued from her husband Willy's influence and published under her own name.

An asterisk in the text denotes a name or place identified in the end notes.

*

I am indebted for some of the factual information here to Judith Thurman's comprehensive and highly readable biography *Secrets of the Flesh, A Life of Colette* (Alfred A. Knopf Inc., New York, 1999; Bloomsbury Publishing Plc, London, 1999), and for the following references:

(1) Thurman, p 411
(2) Thurman, pp 419 and 457
(3) Thurman, p 460
(4) Thurman, p 104

THE SOLDIER'S HAT

I have occasionally mentioned, as I remember it, Paul Masson, known as Lemice-Térieux—*Le Mystérieux.** A former judge in Pondicherry in India, a brilliant—and dangerous—hoaxer, his work linked him with the Catalogue of Early Printed Books at the *Bibliothèque Nationale*. It was through him, through his connection with the *Bibliothèque*, that I made the acquaintance of the woman whose unique adventure in love I am about to relate.

The mature man Paul Masson and the very young woman I then was formed over a period of some eight years quite a firm friendship. Not a jolly man himself, Paul Masson made it his business to keep me cheerful and amused. I think that, seeing me very much alone and housebound, he pitied me, although he kept that hidden; and also, I think he took a measure of pride in being so easily able to make me laugh. We often used to dine together in the little third floor apartment in the rue Jacob, I in the flowing dressing gown I liked to imagine made me a Botticelli-like figure, he always in a black suit, fusty and correct. With his reddish goatee beard, faded complexion and half-closed eyes, his lack of distinctive features made one think he was in camouflage. Though friendly enough, he never used the familiar *tu* to me, and whenever he abandoned his carefully controlled impersonality, showed all the signs of a very good education. He never sat down to write anything, while we were alone together, in the office-study of the person I call "*Monsieur* Willy", and I do not remember that he ever, over the course of several years, asked me an indiscreet question.

On the other hand, his caustic manner enchanted me. I admired the way he was prepared at any moment to be aggressive in the most measured of tones, without ever actually becoming heated. And he would carry up to my third floor, in addition to anecdotes about Parisian life, a string of ingenious falsehoods which I loved as if they were fairy stories or fantastical tales. If he ran into Marcel Schwob,* what joyous good fortune for me! The two men pretended to hate one another, made a game of exchanging insults with the greatest of courtesy, in restrained voices. Schwob hissed his sibilants between clenched teeth, Masson, with little coughs, spat out venom like an old lady. Then they declared peace, gossiped at length and I warmed myself in the glow of those two fine and devious minds.

The considerable leisure hours granted Paul Masson by the *Bibliothèque Nationale* guaranteed me an almost daily visit, whilst the sparky conversation of Schwob was a rarer treat. Alone with the cat and Masson, I was not obliged to talk at all and this prematurely aged man could relax in silence. He would often make jottings about heaven knows what in the pages of a notebook with black moleskin covers. The coal-burning stove spread a carbonaceous torpor over our idleness, we would listen sleepily to the gun-shot crash of the street door, I would rouse myself to eat sugared sweets or salted nuts, and I would call on my guest, who was perhaps, whilst keeping himself quite private, the most devoted of my friends, to make me laugh. I was twenty-two, my recent illness left me looking like an anaemic cat, and my hair, which I had let grow until it measured a full one metre fifty-eight, I would undo and allow to fall in a flowing wave to my feet.

'Paul, tell me some lies.'

'Which lies would you like?'

'Any. How is your family?'

'*Madame*, you forget that I am a bachelor.'

'But you told me…'

'Ah! Yes, I remember. My illegitimate daughter is very well. For her Sunday outing I took her to lunch on the edge of town, in a garden. The rain had glued big yellow leaves from a lime tree to the metal table top. She had great fun peeling them off and we ate lukewarm chips, with our feet on the soaking gravel…'

'No, no, not that, it's too sad. I like the lady in the library better.'

'What lady? We idlers don't employ any.'

'The one who's working on a novel set in India, among the Hindus… or so you told me.'

'It's meant to be serialised in the papers. She's still

toiling at it. Today I was grand and generous, I gave her some *baobabs*, some palm trees taken from life, a *fakir*, a handful of formulaic incantations, *Maharathis*,* howler monkeys, Sikhs, saris and rupees by the lakh…'*

Rubbing one dry hand against the other, he added: 'She gets one *sou* per line.'

'One *sou!*' I exclaimed. 'Why one *sou?*'

'Because she works for a fellow who gets two *sous* a line and who works for a fellow who gets four *sous* a line, and he works for a fellow who gets ten *sous* a line.'

'But what you're telling me must surely be one of your lies?'

'Not everything can be lies,' Masson sighed.

'What's her name?'

'She calls herself, as a first name, Marco, as you might have guessed, since women of a certain age have little choice, when they belong to the arts world. They have to be something like Marco, Léo, Ludo, Aldo… all this we owe to the good George Sand…'

'Of a certain age? She's old then?'

Paul Masson's glance towards my face, which became childlike again when it was surrounded by my long hair, was hard to decipher.

'Yes,' he said.

Then he corrected himself, his voice more formal: 'Forgive me, I was in error. No, I meant to say. No, she is not old.'

I was exultant.

'You see? You see, that's a lie since you haven't even chosen an age for her!'

'If you insist…' said Masson.

'Or else the lady is your mistress and your name Marco is just a disguise.'

'I do not need Mme Marco. I have a mistress who is, thank God, my housekeeper.'

He looked at his watch, rose to his feet.

'You must give your husband my apologies, I have to get back before the omnibuses stop running. As for the very real Mme Marco, I will introduce you to her whenever you express the wish to meet her.'

He reeled off, very rapidly: 'She is the wife of the painter V… a school friend of mine who made her dreadfully unhappy. She fled the marital home where her all-round perfection had made her impossible. She is still beautiful, full of wit and without a penny. She lives in a boarding house in rue Demours, where she pays four twenty-five francs a month for bed and breakfast. She scrapes a living by writing—serialised stories, uncredited, page-fillers for the papers—and by addressing envelopes. She gives English lessons at three francs an hour and has never had a lover. You can see that the lie is as unpleasant as the truth.'

I handed back to him the lighted Pigeon lamp* and accompanied him to the staircase. As he was going down, the little flame gave his beard a red glow from underneath, highlighting the way it turned up slightly at its tip.

When I had had enough of hearing about "Marco", I asked Paul Masson to introduce us, and not by bringing her to rue Jacob. He had given me to understand that she was roughly twice my age, and I told myself it was more appropriate for a young woman to make the effort if she wished to meet a lady less young than herself. Naturally, Paul Masson accompanied me to rue Demours.

The boarding house where Mme Marco V… lived has now been demolished. Around 1897, this detached villa had retained of its former garden only a spindle tree hedge, a gravel drive, and five steps up to its front door. As soon as I set foot in the hall a feeling of sadness enveloped me. For certain smells, I won't say culinary, but redolent of kitchens, are the dreadful indicators of poverty. On the first floor, Paul Masson knocked at a door and the voice of Mme Marco bade us enter. A voice that was just right, neither too sharp nor too serious, bright and nicely modulated… what a surprise! Mme Marco seemed young, Mme Marco was attractive, wore a silk dress, Mme Marco had pretty eyes, almost black, and slender like a doe's, a little groove at the tip of her nose, hair touched with henna, tightly curled, making a thick roll on her forehead, like the Queen of England, falling to short ringlets on her neck in the manner, called "eccentric", of some female painters or musicians.

She called me "young *madame*", said that she had heard a lot about me—and my long hair—from Masson, apologised, without fuss, for having no port or sweets to offer me. She indicated with a simple wave of the arm the place where she lived and her gesture showed me the scrap of *moquette* that covered a pedestal table, the shiny material of the solitary armchair, and on the two upright chairs two small round cushions of Algerian pattern, threadbare. There was also a carpet of sorts on the floor… the mantelpiece served as her bookshelf.

'There should have been a clock there, but I've locked it away in the cupboard,' said Marco. 'But I assure you it deserved to be. Fortunately I have another cupboard where I can keep my bowl and jug for washing. Do you smoke?'

I shook my head, and Marco moved towards the window to light her cigarette. Then I saw that her silk dress had become thin where it folded. The small amount of linen showing at her neck was very white. Marco and Masson smoked and chatted together, Mme Marco having instantly understood that I preferred to listen rather than to speak. I forced myself not to look at the wallpaper, with its stripes of old gold and crimson, nor at the bed and its counterpane of cotton damask.

'Take a look at that small painting instead, there,' Mme Marco told me. 'It's by my husband. It's so pretty I kept it. It's that little place in Hyères, you remember, Masson.'

And I considered with envy Marco, Masson and the small canvas, which had all been to Hyères… like most young people, I knew how to withdraw into myself, detached from those talking around me, then to rejoin them in a quick mental leap, then to leave them again. For the entire duration of my visit, thanks to Marco's delicate tact which spared me the business of questions and responses, I could come and go without moving, could observe and close my eyes. I saw her as she was, prompting in me both sorrow and pleasure, for if the regularity of her features was attractive, she had what they call a coarse skin, somewhat grainy, masculine, with red patches here and there on the neck and under the ears. But at the same time I could delight in the vivacity of her intelligent smile, the shape of her doe eyes, the exceptionally proud carriage of the head, free of all affectation. Rather than looking like a pretty woman, she resembled one of those fine and upstanding aristocrats who embellished the eighteenth century and were not ashamed of their beauty. She resembled in particular, Masson told me, her grandfather, the knight of Saint-George, a dazzling ancestor who has no part in my story.

We became friends, Marco and I. And after she had finished her Hindu novel—something similar to *The Woman Who Kills*, or so decided the person who was paid ten *sous* a line—M. Willy eased her financial vulnerability by asking her to do some librarianship tasks for him in return for which she accepted a modest fee, and consented, when I pressed her, to share an impromptu meal with us. I had only to watch her to learn the finest of table manners. M. Willy professed to love all marks of distinction and in Marco had plenty to admire, given her charming manners and her turn of mind, which was courteous without being free and easy, and just a touch sharp. Born twenty years later, she would have made, I believe, a good journalist. When summer came, it was M. Willy who suggested taking this extremely amiable companion, so dignified in her poverty, with us to stay in a village in the hills of the Franche-Comté. The luggage she brought with her was meagre enough to rend one's heart. But at that time I had very little money myself, and we set ourselves up as best we could in a simple, single-storey, echoing inn. The wooden balcony and a wicker armchair were quite enough for Marco, who hardly ever walked. She was more than happy just to relax, to enjoy the vivid crimson skies of evening in the mountains, the overflowing bowls of raspberries. She had travelled, and made comparisons between the valleys that dusk hollowed out here and other landscapes she had seen. Up in these hills, I noticed that Marco received no mail apart from the picture postcards Masson sent her, and the "Best wishes for a happy holiday", again on a postcard, she received from a fellow drudge at the *Bibliothèque Nationale*.

On warm afternoons, under the shade of the awning, Marco would attend to her mending. She sewed badly, but carefully, and it flattered my vanity to give her advice, such as: 'The thread you're using is too thick for fine needles… you shouldn't use blue cotton for chemises, pink is prettier for underthings and against the skin.' I did not hesitate to give her other tips, concerning her face powder, the colour of her lipstick, a harsh pencil with which she emphasised the attractive line of her eyelids. 'Do you think so? Do you think so?' she said. My youthful authority never relented. I took the comb, I opened a graceful little gap in her rolled fringe, I proved my expertise at adding to her gaze a more dark and misty aura, at bringing to her high cheekbones, near the eyes, a faint dawn blush. But I did not know what to do about the thankless skin of her neck, nor a long crease that shadowed her cheek. The flattering glow I had given her face transformed her so thoroughly that I immediately rubbed it off. Under the amber tint of her powder, and better fed than in Paris, she became, with moderation, more animated. She described one of her voyages from previous times, when like a good artist's wife she accompanied her husband from Greek town to Moroccan village, washed out the brushes and fried aubergines and peppers in olive oil. She suddenly laid down her sewing to light a cigarette and blew the smoke from her soft herbivore's nostrils. But she told me the names of sites of interest, not of friends, described inconveniences and not griefs, and I did not dare ask for more. The mornings she used for writing the first chapters of a new novel at a *sou* per line, which the lack of research material, on the subject of the early Christians, seriously hindered.

'Once I've put some lions in the arena, added a blonde virgin captured by the soldiers and an exodus of Christians driven before a storm,' Marco said, 'that's as far as my personal erudition will take me, and for the rest I'll wait until I'm back in Paris.'

I have said: we became friends. That is true, if friendship is defined by a perfect understanding, rare in itself, by the exercise of great tact, carefully disguised, by a deliberate blunting of all sharp points and edges. I could only gain by imitating Marco and her outward appearance of being a "lady". Besides, she never inspired in me any wish to challenge her. I could sense her as she was, whole and clear-cut, repelled by anything that might cause harm, withdrawn from all forms of feminine competition. But the difference in ages, which love makes light of, is more sensitive when it comes to friendship, especially between two women, especially when the friendship is just beginning and would like, as with love, to grab with both hands. Being in the country filled me with a terrible desire for flowing waters, wet meadows, for shifting backdrops to one's idleness…

'Marco, you don't feel like getting up early tomorrow, going to spend the morning among the pine trees where there are wild cyclamen and purple mushrooms?'

Marco shuddered, wrung her small hands together: 'Oh, no…! Oh, no…! You go. You go by yourself, frisky young goat…'

For I forgot to say that M. Willy, after the first week, had returned to Paris "on business". He wrote me short notes.

He ornamented his prose, which drew on Mallarmé* and Fénéon,* with onomatopoeias inscribed in Greek characters, quotations directly from the German and loving expressions in English…

So I climbed up towards the pine trees and cyclamens by myself. The contrast between a burning sun and the lingering, night-chilled coolness of the mossy grasses was enough to turn me giddy. More than once I thought of not going back for lunch. But I returned because of Marco, who savoured the complete rest as if she needed to rid herself of a weariness built up over twenty years. Rest which she took with her eyes closed, pale beneath her powder, with the air of one overwhelmed or of a convalescent. At the end of the afternoon she walked a little way along the road which, even when it ran through the village, barely amounted to more than a winding forest track, an admirable track that made a satisfying crunch under one's feet.

It should not be imagined that the other "tourists" were much more active than ourselves. People of my age can remember that a summer in the country, around 1897, was not at all like the active, bustling holidays of today. A cold stream, pure and pebbly, made a fine destination for the walks of the most energetic, who carried with them folding chairs, a piece of sewing, a novel, afternoon tea, useless fishing rods. On evenings when the moon was full, after dinner—the bell for which rang at seven—young women and men went off in groups along the road, turned round, retraced their steps, halted and wished each other good evening. 'How about taking bicycles and going to Saut-de-Giers tomorrow?—Oh, we don't make plans like that. It depends on the weather…'

The men wore tight-fitting waistcoats, with two rows of false buttons, under a jacket of black or cream alpaca, chequered caps or a straw hat. The girls and young women were plump, greedy, in dresses of white linen or raw Indian silk. When they rolled back their sleeves you could see white arms, and beneath the wide-brimmed hats the suntan never rose as far as the forehead. Adventurous families practised what they called "bathing", immersing themselves in the afternoons in a widened-out part of the river, a kilometre or so from the village. In the evenings, around the *table d'hôte*, the children's wet hair smelled of the dank pool and of wild mint.

One day when my mail was particularly plentiful: two letters, an article cut from *Art et Critique* and some other odds and ends, Marco, to let me read in peace, assumed her convalescent's attitude, closed her eyes, leant her head on the raffia headrest of the wicker chair. She was wearing the raw cotton dressing gown she put on to spare the rest of her wardrobe when we were alone in our bedrooms or on the wooden balcony. It was when she donned this dressing gown that she belonged faithfully to her era and her age, as could be seen from a particular series of clues, both flattering and melancholy, such as a certain, unintended wave in her hair which accentuated the narrowness of her temples, a certain short fringe which would never allow itself to be combed in a different direction, a way of holding her chin that was forced on her by a stiffened collar, knees pressed together and never crossed, the ill-advised dressing gown itself which instead of being content to remain a simple working garment was tricked out in false lace at the neck, the cuffs, and folds of drapery at the hips…

These indications of era and of character my own generation was in the process of repudiating. The new hairstyle of glittering strands, as worn coiled round the head by Cléo de Mérode,* took its cue from the halo effect of a boatman's straw hat, then there were shirt-blouses in the English style and straight skirts. Bicycles and bloomers had reached all classes. I was beginning to be infatuated with starched linen collars, sturdy woollens from England. The divergence between the two fashions, the recent and the brand new, was too striking not to be a humiliation for women short of money, who were slow in adopting one and abandoning the other. Sometimes, keeping my enthusiasm for the new and my vanity in check, I suffered for the heroic Marco in two worn-out dresses and two pale blouses…

I slowly folded my letters, my attention never leaving the woman feigning sleep, the pretty woman of 1870, 1875, who refused, out of modesty and out of indigence, to follow us into 1898… with the intransigence of young women, I said to myself: "In Marco's place, I would do my hair like this, I would dress like that…" Then I made excuses for her: "But she has no money. If I had more money, I would help her…"

Marco heard me folding my letters, opened her eyes and smiled: 'How's your post? All good?'

'Yes, Marco,' I said, and I risked asking her: 'Is yours not sent on here?'

'Oh, it is. I don't get any mail except what you see delivered.'

As I said nothing, she went on all in a rush: 'I am, as you know, separated from my husband. The friends of V… have remained, thank God, his friends and not mine. I had a child, twenty years ago, and I lost him when he was very young. And I have never had a lover. Everything is very simple, as you can see.'

'Never had a lover…' I repeated.

Marco laughed at my look of consternation.

'Is that the thing that strikes you most? You needn't look so surprised. It came so low on the list of things to think about that in the end I didn't think about it at all.'

My gaze wandered from her beautiful eyes, at rest now in the pure air and the green of the chestnut groves, to the little crease at the end of her intelligent nose, to her teeth, slightly off-white but healthy and even: 'But you're very pretty, Marco!'

'Oh!' she said gaily, 'I was even charming once. If I hadn't been, V… wouldn't have married me. To tell the truth, I'm convinced fate has spared me a major disadvantage: being what they call highly emotional. No, no. Blood rising to one's cheeks, pupils rolling in passion, nostrils quivering, I admit I've never known and never missed any of that. You believe me, don't you?'

'Yes, yes,' I said mechanically, looking at Marco's mobile nostrils.

She laid her narrow hand on mine, with a freedom which, I knew, did not come to her easily: 'Much poverty, my child, and before poverty the job of being an artist's wife, with everything that means in terms of… sheer manual labour, closer to the job of being a general household drudge… I wonder how I'd have found the time to be idle, cossetted, secretly elegant, running off to assignations—to have a love life in short…'

She sighed, stroked a hand over my hair, pushed it back

towards my temples.

'Why don't you show more of your face? When I was young I had my hair this way…'

And as I hated having my alley-cat's bony temples exposed, I avoided her small hand, I interrupted Marco, exclaiming: 'Oh, no, certainly not! I'm going to do *your* hair, I've got a brilliant idea!'

Brief exchanges of confidence, pastimes of a pair of recluses, resembling the superficial conversations of a convent workroom or else the empty leisure of a convalescent, I do not recall our agreeable holiday giving rise to any real intimacy. I was drawn into a feeling of deference towards Marco, but in contradiction, to care almost nothing for her opinions on matters concerning the real world or the world of feelings. When she used to tell me she could have been my mother, I realised that our good relations would never resemble my true, impassioned, daughterly sentiments. But at that period, I had no girl or woman friend of my own age with whom I could be gay and carefree, with whom I could share a wordless complicity, a liveliness expressed in wild fits of laughter, or even indulge in those physical rivalries and somewhat brutal pleasures that Marco's age, her delicate complexion and her character made impossible for her and for me.

We talked, we read too. I had read randomly and voraciously in my childhood. Marco had educated herself. At first I thought I could draw on Marco's well-furnished memory and mind whatever the occasion. But I noticed that she answered with a certain listlessness, and as if not sure of her own words.

'Marco, why do you call yourself Marco?'

'Because my name is Léonie,' she replied, 'and that was no name for the wife of V… when I was twenty, V… had me pose in a Greek cap with a tassel, tipped over one ear, and Turkish slippers. As he painted, he sang this old love song:

'Do you love, Marco la Belle,
Dancing, light, in flower'd halls…
Do you like, in night's sweet shade…
Ta na na, ta na na na…

'I have forgotten the rest…'

I had never heard Marco sing. Her voice was precise, on the faint side, piping, like the voices of some elderly men.

'They were still singing that when I was young,' she said. 'Artists' studios have done a great deal to propagate bad music…'

All she seemed to want to retain from her younger days was a shallow kind of irony… I was too young to discern in her the serenity and contented modesty that comes from abnegation.

Towards the end of our Franche-Comté holiday, however, something astonishing happened to Marco. Her husband, who was painting in North America, had his lawyer send her a cheque for fifteen thousand francs. Her only reaction was to comment, with a laugh: 'He has a lawyer these days? Goodness!'

Then she returned to their envelope both cheque and lawyer's letter and made no further reference to them. But at dinner a certain feverishness came over her and she asked the waitress, *sotto voce*, if we could have some champagne. And we did. It was sweet and tepid, with a faint flavour of cork and we only drank half the bottle between us.

Before closing the communicating door between us as we did every evening Marco asked me in a distracted manner a number of questions: 'Do you think people will still be wearing, next winter, those velvet coats with wide sleeves, you know the ones I mean? Where did that charming hat you were wearing last spring come from, with the brim raised like a roof? I liked it very much—on you I mean…'

She spoke lightly, scarcely seemed to listen to my replies and I pretended not to guess how deeply she had concealed her hunger and her thirst for clothes that would do her credit and for fresh new linens.

By the following morning she was her usual self.

'All in all,' she told me 'I don't see why I should accept the money which that… well, my husband… is offering me. If it suits him, at this juncture, to hand out alms, it doesn't mean I have to accept them…'

As she spoke she picked at threads loosened by the laundress' ministrations from the very ordinary lace that bordered her dressing gown, in whose opening appeared a chemise modest in the extreme. I grew irritated and I scolded Marco as an older person would have rebuked a little girl. To the point where I felt a little ashamed, but she laughed: 'There, there, don't get angry! Since you wish it, I shall allow myself to be kept by my lord V… it's certainly my turn.'

I leant my cheek against Marco's. Together we sat and watched the rugged, ruddy disc of the rising sun reach its zenith, drinking up all the shadows that lay between the mountains. The bends in the river trembled in the distance.

Marco sighed: 'Would it cost a lot, a pretty little suspender belt and corset with rococo roses on the tips of the garters…?'

*

Our return to Paris reunited Marco with her serialised novel. Once again I beheld her hat with its three blue thistles, her faded black dress, her dark grey gloves and her schoolgirl's satchel, so-called leather but made of cardboard. Before thinking about improving the elegance of her own person, she wanted to change where she lived and took a year's rent on a furnished two-room apartment on the ground floor, with a bathroom and some sort of kitchen arrangement, shut away in a cupboard. It was dark in broad daylight, but the cretonne hangings round the bed and at the windows, white and red, were not in too bad a condition. Marco took her midday sustenance at a teashop near the Library, and in the evenings ate tea and *tartines* at home, unless I could manage to keep her with me, around a table on which stuffed olives and rollmops replaced soup and roast. Sometimes Paul Masson brought from Quillet, the *pâtissier*'s in rue Buci, an excellent chocolate "*Quillet*".

Abandoning herself to her literary task, Marco had so far only acquired, October proving wet, a sort of rubberised three-quarter length mackintosh which smelt of tar. One day she turned up, anxiety painted in her eyes, a guilty doe.

'Look,' she said. 'I've come to be scolded. I think I bought this coat too quickly, I get the impression that this… that this isn't quite the thing.'

Her timid demeanour, like a younger sister's, made me laugh, but I desisted when I examined the coat. A reliable instinct drew Marco, in other ways so discerning, towards poor materials, deplorable tailoring, regrettable accessories…

The very next day, I made the time to go out with her and to fit her out properly. Neither she nor I was inclined towards *haute couture*, but I had the pleasure of seeing Marco looking slender and young again in a dark suit, a serge dress of navy blue with a white bib front. With a short coat in *karakul* fur, two hats and assorted lingerie, it all came, if you please, to fifteen hundred francs: as one can see, I had not been mean with the funds sent by the painter V…

I could easily have found fault with Marco's hair. But just that season a change was taking place in the volume and arrangement of hair, and Marco was able to appear ahead of the trend. In which I sincerely envied her, for my long hair, whether I twined it "Ceres-fashion"* round my head, or let it fall to the hem of my skirt—"like a rope down a well", Jules Renard* used to say—cast a shadow over my existence.

Here I come to the memory of a particular evening… M. Willy having business to attend to, Marco, Paul Masson and I remained alone together after dinner. Left to ourselves, the three of us customarily became full of secret glee, a trifle childish and as it were reassured. Masson sometimes read out loud from the serial in the newspaper, a novel overflowing with haughty countesses, costumed balls in winter gardens, carriages dashing off "at full gallop", drawn by pure-bloods, young girls exposed to a thousand dangers, pale but resolute. And we would laugh happily.

'Ah!' Marco would sigh. 'I'll never be able to write like that. As far as serialised fiction goes, I'll never be more than a minor amateur.'

'Well, minor amateur,' Masson said one evening, 'here's your opening. I found it in the personal column: "Man of letters, well-known name, offers guidance to would-be authors of both sexes."'

'Both sexes!' Marco said. 'I'll pass on that, Masson. I only have one, and even then I think I may be exaggerating.'

'Then I shall move on,' Masson said, 'to "Lieutenant, regular army, garrisoned near Paris, sensitive, cultivated, seeks correspondence with woman of wit and heart". All very good, but this soldier, it seems, only wants a pen-friend. Nevertheless, shall we write? Let's write. The best letter wins a box of Kohler's Gianduja,* with hazelnuts.'

'If it's a big box,' I said, 'then count me in. How about you Marco?'

Her nose and its little crease bent over a writing pad, Marco was already at work. Masson produced twenty or so lines of sly obscenity mixed with humour. I came to a standstill on the first page out of pure laziness. But what a pretty letter Marco had produced by comparison!

'First prize!' I cried.

'Pearls before swine…' Masson murmured. 'Shall we send it? *Poste restante*. Alex 2, box 59. Give it to me, I'll see to it.'

'What harm can it do?' said Marco.

Our evening's amusements over, she put her raincoat on again, stood at the mirror to arrange the narrow hat—this one my choice—which made her head so small and her eyes so big beneath its turned-down rim. 'There she is,' she exclaimed. 'There she is, the mature woman who seduces sensitive and cultivated lieutenants!'

Pigeon lamp in hand, she preceded Masson to the door.

'I'll hardly see you this week,' she told me. 'I have two chores to complete: a chariot race, and Christians in the lion's den.'

'Haven't I read that somewhere before…?' Masson said insinuatingly.

'I certainly hope so,' Marco retorted. 'If it hadn't already been done by everyone, how would I do my research?'

The following week, Masson brought along a copy of the newspaper, and with his hard and fluted fingernail pointed to three lines in the *Personal column* section: "*Alex 25 begs author of delightful letter beginning* '*How presumptuous*' *to send address. Discretion guaranteed.*"

'Marco,' he said, you've not just won the box of Gianduja, but also, as Pierre Veber* says, you've hit the jackpot.'

Marco shrugged her shoulders.

'It was cruel, what you made me do. He's going to think someone's laughing at him, that poor boy.'

Masson narrowed his eyes into their most inquisitorial look: 'Feeling sorry for him already, my dear!'

These memories are distant but clear. They emerge from the inevitable mists that shroud the long days of that same period, the monotony of the entertainments, dress rehearsals and suppers at Pousset's, my alternating moods of animal high spirits and deep woe, the splitting of myself between a terrified wildness and a great capacity for self-delusion. But they are mists which leave the faces of friends unaltered and brightly illuminated.

It is on another rainy day at the end of October or beginning of November that Marco comes to keep me company one evening, I remember the tarry smell of the rubberised raincoat. She kisses me. Her gentle nose is damp, she sighs with relief as she relaxes before the red glow of the stove, she opens her satchel: 'Here, read this,' she said. 'Doesn't he have a nice way of putting things, for a… a simple soldier?'

If I had allowed myself one criticism, on reading it, I would have said: too nice. A letter much worked-over, recopied—a draft, two drafts, thrown in the waste paper basket. The letter of a timid man, faintly poetic like everyone else…

'But Marco, you mean you wrote to him?'

The very proper Marco laughed in my face.

'Charming daughter of M. de La Palisse,* I can't hide anything from you! Wrote? Wrote more than once even! The crime is making me hungry. You don't have a cake, an apple?'

While she delicately nibbled, I showed off my pretensions as a handwriting expert: 'Look, Marco, how carefully your "simple soldier" has camouflaged a word already started. A sign of worldliness, and touchiness too. The writer, as Crépieux-Jamin* says, dislikes being taken for a fool…'

Marco agreed, distractedly. I thought she looked pretty, lively; she glanced at herself in the mirror, pressed her teeth together and spread her lips, a sort of grimace that few women can deny themselves when they stand before a mirror and have white teeth.

'What's that stuff that leaves your gums pinker when you clean your teeth, Colette?'

'*Cherries* something…'

'Thank you, I know, *Cherries toothpaste*. Will you do me a favour? Don't tell Paul Masson about my letter-writing eccentricities. His teasing can go a bit far. I'm not intending to spend enough time on my relations with the regular army for them to become ridiculous. Ah! I was forgetting… my husband has sent another fifteen thousand francs.'

'Well, blow me down, as they say where I come from… and this item of news slipped your mind, just like that?'

'Why, yes,' said Marco. 'Just like that.'

She raised her eyebrows in an expression of surprise, to demonstrate to me, elegantly, that questions of money are always of secondary importance.

*

From that moment on, it seems to me that everything advanced very quickly for Marco. Perhaps it is the effect of distance. One of my house-moves—the first—transposes me from rue Jacob to the upper end of rue de Courcelles, from a dark little dwelling to a top floor studio whose skylight let in heat, cold, an excess of daylight. I want to show what I can do, satisfy some growing—and modest—appetites for luxury: I buy some white goat skin rugs and a kind of bath tub, a folding one, from the Chaboche store.

Marco, a denizen of the half-light, the left bank and of libraries, blinks her pretty eyes beneath the attic studio's skylights, stares at the white divans in faux polar bear, doesn't like my new hairstyle, a tall chignon, twisted down over the forehead: the Golden Helmet fashion was conquering the most respectable of heads…

It would not be worth mentioning such minor comings and goings if they did not serve to explain that, for some time,

I had had no more than fleeting glimpses of Marco, images that flickered rapidly past like the views in a zoetrope. When she brought me the second letter from the sentimental lieutenant, I had crossed a number of bridges. I observed Marco's arrival in my bright new home. I saw that she was distinctly prettier than she had been the year before. She sat on my bear-skin chairs, which left hairs on the seats of all who sat on them. Beneath the hem of her dress a foot peeped out, a slender foot happily wearing the shoe it deserved. She sometimes looked down at her gloved hand, sometimes around the unfamiliar apartment, through the half-veil neatly stretched over the little furrow at the end of her nose, but she did not appear to see either the one or the other at all clearly. She waited with a playful kind of impatience while I showed off how the curtains worked; she admired the bath, which when opened out, looked vaguely like a vertical coffin. She was so patient and her mind so obviously miles away that eventually I noticed and I asked her unceremoniously: 'By the way, Marco, how's the simple soldier?'

She met my gaze with eyes softened by make-up and myopia: 'He's very well, as it happens. His letters are charming, definitely.'

'Definitely? How many have you received?'

'Three in all. I'm beginning to think that's enough. Don't you agree?'

'No, since they're charming and they amuse you.'

'I dislike having to use the *poste restante* office. It's not a nice place… everyone looks as if they're guilty of something… here, if you're interested…'

She tossed on to my lap a letter she was holding, folded

and ready, in her gloved hand. I read through it somewhat slowly, so impressed was I by her serious tone, devoid of any humour.

'What an exceptional lieutenant you've stumbled on here, Marco! I'm sure that if he wasn't held back by his timidity…'

'Timidity?' Marco protested. 'He's already hoping for our exchange of letters to be less anonymous! What cheek! For a timid fellow…'

She broke off to raise her demi-veil, beneath which her coarse-grained skin was becoming warm, and red spots appearing on her cheeks. But by now she knew how to apply powder with skill, to enliven her mouth with a little colour. Instead of a downtrodden woman of forty-five, I now had before me a dashing forty-year-old, chin held high, above the stiffened collar that concealed the secrets of her neck. Once more, thanks to her very beautiful eyes, forgetting the alterations to the rest of her face, I sighed to myself: 'What a shame…'

Our new lodgings threw us both a little out of our usual routines, I saw Marco rather less often. But she still occupied my thoughts a good deal. The affectionate balance, which between two women friends confers authority on one and a willingness to be advised on the other, turned me into a demanding young guide. I decided that Marco should wear shorter skirts, have a tighter waist. I proscribed decorative braids that were ageing, colours that dated one, and in particular forbade certain hats, which on Marco, mysteriously and irremediably condemned her. She allowed herself to be led, hesitating for a moment: 'Do you think so? Are you sure?' and from the corner of her eye her lovely pupil would slide towards me.

We liked to meet in a little tea room on the corner of rue de l'Echelle and rue d'Argenteuil, a "British" establishment, narrow, hot, impregnated with the sharp aroma of Ceylon. We "took tea" like the self-indulgent ladies of those distant times, with toast and plenty of cakes to follow. I liked my tea very strong, generously whitened with cream and very sweet. I used to believe I was learning English when I asked the waitress: '*Edith, please, a little more milk, and butter…*'

It was at this little "British" place that I noticed a change in Marco, as striking as if, in the course of a few days, she had turned blonde, or become a drug addict. I feared some new danger, I imagined the wicked husband had reasserted his power over a frightened woman… but if frightened, she would not have that same look in her eyes, as her restless gaze swept the room from table to walls, inexpressive, profoundly indifferent to everything it alighted on…

'Marco…? Marco!'

'Dear friend?'

'Well, Marco, what is it? Has your ship come in? Another fifteen thousand? Or what?'

She smiled at me as if I were a stranger.

'My ship…? No.'

She emptied her teacup without pausing for breath and softly murmured: 'Oh! That was silly, I've burned my mouth…'

Consciousness of her surroundings and her natural gentleness resurfaced from the far-away depths of her eyes. She saw on my own face a look of astonishment, and she blushed in her particular way, inelegantly, unevenly.

'Sorry!' she said, placing her small hand on mine.

She sighed, relaxed: 'Ah!' she said. 'What luck there's no one here… I am a little… what shall I say… not quite myself.'

'Another cup? Good and hot…'

'No, no… I think it's the port I had before I came here. No, nothing, thank you.'

She leant back in her chair and closed her eyes. She was wearing her newest costume; a small oval brooch of the family heirloom type fastened the stiff collar of her cream blouse tight at the neck. The next moment she was animated again, natural, consulting the mirror in her brand new bag and keen to confess before I had even begun to question her: 'Ah! I'm better now! It's that port, I'm certain of it. Yes, my dear, port! And in the company of Lieutenant Alexis Trallard, son of General Trallard.'

'Oh!' I exclaimed, relieved. 'Is that all it was? You frightened me. So, you've seen this simple soldier! What's he like? Is he like his letters? Does he stammer? Does he lisp? Is he bald? Has he a wine stain on his nose?'

With these and similar frivolities, my intention was to make Marco laugh; but she listened with a distinguished and dreamy look on her face, nibbling at a piece of toast gone cold.

'My dear,' she said in the end, 'if you'd let me get a word in, I'd be able to inform you that Lieutenant Trallard is neither a cripple nor a monster either. Which, as it happens, I knew beforehand because in his letter last week he enclosed a photograph.'

She took my hand: 'Don't be angry. I didn't dare mention it to you. I was scared.'

'Of what?'

'Of you, dearest, of being mocked a little. And then,

simple straightforward fear.'

'But why fear?'

Her arms gestured ignorance, apology, then crossed defensively over her chest.

'I have the thing here,' she said, and opened her bag. 'It is, naturally, very poor, just a snapshot.'

'He's a lot better-looking than his photograph—naturally?'

'Better, my goodness… he is very different. Especially the expression.'

As I bent over the portrait, so did she, as if to protect it from too stark a judgement.

'Lieutenant Trallard does not have that shadow on his cheek that looks like a sabre cut. The nose, too, is not as long. He has chestnut hair and a moustache that's almost blond.'

After a silence, Marco added timidly: 'He is tall.'

I realised that it was my turn to speak: 'But he's a fine-looking man! Why, he looks like a proper lieutenant, with a physique to match! But what a wonderful story, Marco! And his eyes? What colour are his eyes?'

'Light brown, like his hair,' said Marco with a surge of enthusiasm.

She controlled herself: 'That's to say, as far as I've been able to tell.'

I concealed my surprise at finding opposite me a Marco whose words, whose embarrassment, whose naïvety exceeded anything a young filly taking a glass of port with a lieutenant would have felt. I would never have thought that behind the façade of a mature woman, married, experienced at living amongst artists, I would discover a timorous novice. I resisted saying so to Marco, but I think she understood me all the same, for she attempted to turn her encounter, her discomfort and her lieutenant into a joke. I helped her in this as best I could.

'And when will you be seeing Lieutenant Trallard again, Marco?'

'Not straightaway, I think…'

'Why?'

'Well, because it's good to make him wait and fret a little! Let him simmer!' Marco decreed, lifting a learned finger. 'Simmer! That's the principle I work on!'

We laughed at last, a great deal, rather foolishly. That hour stands out in my memory like the last stop, the last pause at the top of the stairs, where my friend Marco halts, regaining her breath. In the days that followed, I can picture myself working (I signed nothing with my own name either) on the thin, crackling American paper I liked better than any other, and Marco also busy with her work, at a *sou* a line. One afternoon, she comes to see me again.

'Good news about your soldier, Marco?'

She surreptitiously signals "yes, yes" with her chin and one eye, because M. Willy is on the other side of the glazed door. She brings a dress sample for me to inspect, for my approval is essential. She is in excellent spirits, and I think that like a sensible woman she has reduced Lieutenant Alexis Trallard to his proper level of importance. But alone together in my bedroom, my refuge carpeted with mats that smell of damp reeds, she hands me a letter without a word and without a word I read it and hand it back. For words of love call for no response but silence, and the letter I have read is full of love. Gravely, vernally, full of love. Why did that remark, the very one I should have guarded against, escape me? I said, thinking of the freshness of the words I had just read, of the respect underlying them, I said, unwisely: 'How old is he?'

Marco covered her face with both hands, gulped, a brief sob, murmured: 'My God! It's awful…!'

Almost immediately she mastered herself, lowered her hands and said, in harsh and reproachful tones: 'It's gone beyond a joke. I'm having dinner with him tonight.'

She tried to dry her wet eyes, I stopped her.

'Let me, Marco.'

With my two thumbs, I lifted her eyelids carefully towards the eyebrows so that the two tears ready to fall were reabsorbed and the mascara on the lashes did not dissolve in contact with them.

'There! Wait, I haven't finished yet.'

I re-did all her make-up. Her mouth trembled a little. She submitted patiently, sighing as if I were bandaging her. Finally, I refilled her powder puff with a more definite pink powder. Neither of us spoke to one another.

'Whatever happens,' I told her, 'don't cry. At all costs, don't let tears get the better of you.'

She pulled up short at that, laughed: 'After all, this isn't the break-up scene, is it!'

I led her over to the mirror that had the best light. Standing before her reflection, Marco trembled at the corners of her mouth.

'Is that good, Marco?'

'Too good.'

'No such thing as too good. You'll tell me what happens? When?'

'As soon as I find out myself,' Marco said.

Two days later, she was back, despite a spell of turbulent weather, quite warm, which rattled the metal damper in the flue and blew the smoke and the smell of coal back down into the stove.

'Out in this gale, Marco?'

'No bother to me, I've got a cab down in the street.'

'Wouldn't you rather have dinner with me?'

'I couldn't,' she said, turning her head aside.

'Fine. But you can send the kerb-crawler away, it's only half past six. You've plenty of time.'

'No, I don't have time. How's my face?'

'Good. Very good, even.'

'Yes, but… quick, please! Do the same as you did the other day. And then, what's the best thing to wear if I'm having Alex round to my place? A suit I'd wear in town, would you say? In any case I don't have an indoors dress that's suitable…'

'Marco, you know as well as I do…'

'No,' she interrupted, 'I don't know. It's as if you were telling me I know India because I've written a serial set in the Punjab. Here's the thing, he's having a sort of supper sent round to my apartment… a cold buffet: glazed chicken, champagne, fruits… he says he's like me, he can't stand restaurants… ah, now I think of it, I should have…'

She clapped her hand to her forehead, under the fringe.

'I should have bought that black dress I saw last Saturday at the second-hand shop… exactly my size, with a full skirt and a lace bodice… listen, can you lend me some sheer stockings? It's getting late, I've no time to…'

'Yes, of course, yes, of course…'

'Thank you. Don't you think, a flower to brighten my

dress… no, no flowers in the corsage. Is it true that iris has gone out of fashion as a perfume? It feels as if I've still got heaps of things to ask you… heaps of things…'

Although safely ensconced with me beside the roaring stove, Marco gave me the impression of a woman battered by the wind and rain that lashed the skylight. I seemed to be witnessing a sort of departure, as if Marco were preparing to emigrate, as if a travelling cloak were flapping in the wind about her, a tartan rug being smoothed against the wind.

A figure under siege, soon to be overrun… I could not doubt that an assault was under way against the most helpless of creatures. Silent, as if assisting in the commission of an evil deed, we made haste to get her ready. Marco attempted to laugh it off: 'We're trampling on long-established customs. It's usually the oldest witch who bathes the youngest for the Sabbath…'

'Hush, Marco, don't move, I'll have finished in a minute.'

I rolled up in a paper parcel, along with the pair of silk stockings, a small flask containing some yellow chartreuse.

'Have you any cigarettes at home?'

'Yes. What am I saying? No. But he'll have some on him, he smokes Khedives*…'

'I'm putting four little fancy napkins in the parcel, it's more party-like. Do you want a table cloth as well?'

'No, thank you, I've got an embroidered one which I bought in the old days, at Brousse.'

We were speaking in rapid whispers, not smiling. At the door, Marco turned her face to me, damp, beautifully made up, bewildered, a face in which I could read nothing that resembled joy. My thoughts followed her, in the cab that carried her off through the rain and dark, over cobbles filled with puddles on whose surfaces, under the lamp posts, the wind drew feeble grimaces of laughter. I wanted to open the window to watch her go, but the whole tumultuous night rushed into the room and I shut it again, leaving the traveller to set off on a voyage far from safe, her only ballast a pair of silk stockings, a pink-painted face, a bag of fruit and a bottle of champagne.

I still accorded Lieutenant Trallard no more than a partial reality, although I had seen him pictured in that photograph. A very French face, nose rather long, forehead sharply sculpted, hair *en brosse* and the indispensable moustache… but the image of Marco obscured it, Marco full of anguish, beautiful, enhanced by my artifices, and breathing rapidly, like a quivering deer who thinks she hears a vague noise, the approaching footfalls of a hunting party… I listened to rain and wind, I calculated her chances of crossing town, making a safe landing, coming through it all unharmed: 'She was looking very pretty this evening. I hope the heavy shade on her lamp lets enough light fall on her face… this young man fills her mind, flatters her, peoples her solitude, rejuvenates her, in short…'

A sudden squall of foul weather buffeted the window pane. An oozing black shape, like some little reptile, emerged from the bottom of the window and began to crawl slowly across the floor… from which I realised that the window did not shut properly and that the water was beginning to trickle over the carpet. I went to fetch some floor cloths and the assistance of Maria, the woman from the Aveyron who was my servant at that period. On the way I opened the door to Masson, who had just pressed on the bell three times. While he peeled off a limp rubberised cape which fell dripping on the flagstones like a basketful of eels, I exclaimed: 'Didn't you pass Marco? She's just on her way down. She was sorry she couldn't see you...'

Lies must have the ability to give off their own particular aroma, perceptible to people with heightened senses. Paul Masson sniffed the air in my direction, briefly twitched his goatee beard and disappeared in search of M. Willy in his white-painted workroom, which vaguely resembled—half-length curtains, beaded mouldings and small glass panes—a disused confectioner's.

From this point on, everything moves rapidly for Marco. Yet she came to see me the day after the stormy night and had no confidences to share. Admittedly, the presence of a third party prevented any. That day my thirst to know was held in check by the fear that her confidences might contain something rather dreadful, because of the curiously furtive and punished air that seemed to have taken hold of her. At least, I think that is what I remember. My memories, afterwards, are much clearer. It would be impossible to forget how Marco underwent a magical transformation, a kind of overexcited adolescence, with all its tell-tale signs that no one can mistake. The slightest shock made her start. A thimbleful of Muscat de Frontignan lit fires in her cheeks and eyes. She laughed for no reason, stared into the middle distance as if bemused, constantly took out her powder puff and mirror. Everything was happening very fast. I could not put off for long the "Well, Marco?" that she must have been expecting.

One clear and chilly winter evening, Marco was with me. I loaded the stove with fuel. She kept her gaze firmly fixed on the rosy glow and said nothing.

'Are you warm enough in your little flat, Marco? Is the coal fire adequate?'

She smiled haphazardly, like a deaf person, made no reply and in the end I said: 'So, Marco? Content? Fulfilled?'

It was this last word, the most significant, I think, that she pushed aside with a gesture.

'I did not believe,' she said, speaking very quietly, 'that anything like this could exist…'

'What? Fulfilment?'

She blushed unevenly, in dark, fiery patches. I asked her, taking my turn to be naïve: 'But why don't you look more pleased?'

'Can anyone take pleasure in something terrible, something so like an… an evil spell?'

Privately, I allowed myself to think that employing so dark and heavy a term was overstating the case, or as they say, putting a very big hat on a little head and I waited for what she was going to say next—but she said nothing. At this point follows a short period of silence. I did not see anything wrong in Marco keeping silent about her affair, I was more concerned about the affair itself, thinking—unfairly and with a short memory—that she had been too ready to reward a mere passer-by, even if this passer-by was a military man, son of a general, and with light chestnut hair into the bargain.

When the period of reserve was over, there began the period of enjoyment. A happiness, once acknowledged, is rarely kept private; Marco's happiness, having been accepted, had little to say, confining itself to banalities. I learned that she had met, as does everyone, "someone unique", whose every action showered blessings on the bedazzled lover. I was not allowed to remain ignorant of the fact that as well as a "noble soul", Alexis possessed a "physique of iron". And if Marco did not belong, thank God, to the tribe of overdetailed and boastful whisperers whom I call the How-many-times-a-night ladies, she had an unspoken way of expressing, by embarrassed confusion, by exaggerated reticence, what I would have been all too glad not to know.

This honest victim of late love, of the voluptuous shock, did not immediately abandon herself to the thunderbolt, to untrammelled bliss. But she could not escape the trap her new condition set for her, the most inevitable aspect of which is eloquence, of gesture and of word.

A few weeks at first had the effect of turning her thin, with fevered and splendid eyes. 'A Rops!'* Paul Masson would say when she wasn't there. '*Madame* Chantelouve!' M. Willy added. 'What the devil can our good Marco be up to, to go round looking like that?'

Masson narrowed his small eyes, shrugged a single shoulder. 'Nothing,' he said coldly. 'These are phenomena based on falsity, like an imaginary pregnancy, say. Perhaps our good Marco, like other women, believes she is Satan's betrothed. It's a phase: the joys of hell.'

I hated the way either of the two friends called Mme V… "our good Marco". Neither did I appreciate the absence of warmth in the coldly critical remarks these two disillusioned men exchanged, especially when it concerned friendship, esteem, love.

A great sense of calm came to illuminate Marco's features. Serene once more, she gradually lost the feverish gleam of a damned soul and began to fill out. Her skin appeared more smooth, the breathlessness that betrayed her nervousness and haste had vanished. Her slight increase in weight made her gait as she walked more deliberate and her gestures slower; she smoked lazily.

'New phase,' Masson announced. 'Now she looks like a Marco from the old days, when she had just married V… it's the odalisque phase.'

I come to a period when my own existence, more restless and more work-bound as well, put a long gap between our meetings. I did not turn up unannounced at Marco's, where I feared encountering Lieutenant Trallard only partly—indeed very scantily—dressed, in the tiny set of rooms which had as it were no outer hall or antechamber. Teas deferred, meetings missed: chance kept us apart; then at last brought us together again at my apartment one particularly fine day in June when through the raised skylight of the studio blew both warmth and freshness.

Marco smelt good, Marco was wearing a new dress in black and white stripes, Marco was smiling. Her personal romantic novel had been unfolding for eight months already. She seemed to me to have thickened out considerably, so that the proud way she carried her head no longer offset her chin, and her waist, visibly straining, no longer moved at ease, as last year, within the corded silk belt…

'Splendid, Marco! You look magnificent!'

Her long doe-eyes took on an anxious expression: 'You think I'm plump? Not too much, at least?'

She lowered her gaze, smiled mysteriously: 'A little stoutness does wonders for the bust…'

She had not accustomed me to such remarks, and I think

I was the one who felt embarrassed as if Marco—the same Marco who would keep her door firmly closed when we were staying at the inn in the Franche-Comté: "Don't come in, I'm just putting my dressing gown on!"—had deliberately stripped naked in the middle of my studio sitting room.

A second later I told myself I was lacking both generosity and solidarity, that I should rejoice unreservedly at Marco's happiness. To prove my good will, I exclaimed: 'I bet one of these days I'll find Lieutenant Trallard at my door, standing right behind you! I'm far too broadminded, Marco, to refuse him his tea and cream cheese *tartine*. Agreed?'

Marco sent me a sharp look that made her, for a moment, unrecognisable. Quickly though she turned it aside, she could not prevent me catching the virulent, suspicious glance that surveyed me up and down, my smile, my long hair, everything that youth so readily bestows on a body and face of twenty-five…

'No,' she said.

She remembered herself, gave me her doe-eyed look again: 'It's too soon,' she said gracefully. 'Let's wait and see if the "simple soldier" is worthy of so great a favour!'

But I remained dismayed to have glimpsed, in a look, an untamed female, black with suspicion, hostility and possessive passion. For the first time, the difference in our ages became noticeable to us, hurtful, irremediable. It was the age difference, revealed in the depth of a beautiful velvety eye, that threw our relationship out of kilter, made our easy connection awkward. When I saw Marco again after the day of "the look" and when I enquired after Lieutenant Trallard, the new-style Marco, plump, pale, at ease—we would say nowadays "matronly"—answered me in a new, falsely modest tone of voice, the proprietary tone of a greedy and sated woman. I stared at her in amazement, trying to see what this unexpected and gluttonous love affair had cost her. In vain I searched for that fine and slender figure, the taut waist, the slightly bony and well-sculpted chin, the deep arches beneath which her velvety and almost black eyes were set… she understood I was assessing the change in her, abandoned her regal and well-fed dignity, grew worried: 'What am I to do? I'm getting fat.'

'It's temporary,' I said. 'Do you eat a lot?'

She shrugged her thickened shoulders.

'I don't know. Yes. I'm more greedy, certainly, than… than before. But I've often seen you eat, with no holding back, and you don't get any fatter!'

To excuse myself, I signalled that I couldn't help it. Marco stood up, planted herself in front of the mirror, gripped her waist between her two hands and kneaded it: 'Last year, when I did this, I could feel myself give if I closed my hands together…'

'Last year you were not a happy woman, Marco.'

'Ah! There you have it,' she said grimly.

She examined her reflection at close quarters as if she had been all alone. A few added kilos turned her into another woman, or rather another kind of woman. On her light frame, the flesh distributed itself in uneven and unfortunate ways. "She has a shoemaker's bottom," I thought. Where I come from, they say that the shoemaker, being seated the whole time, develops a flattened posterior, but a square one. "And along with that, breasts like jellyfish, very large and lacking uplift." For a woman, even an affectionate one, judges another woman harshly…

'What?' she said.

'I didn't speak, Marco.'

'Sorry. I thought…'

'If you really want to fight a tendency to put on weight…'

'A tendency,' Marco repeated between her teeth. 'I'll remember that, a tendency.'

'…why not try Swedish gymnastics? People speak highly of it.'

She cast that idea aside with a brusque, intolerant gesture.

'Or cut out breakfast? Fast in the mornings, just have unsweetened lemonade…'

'But I'm hungry in the mornings!' Marco cried. 'Everything has changed, you have to understand! I'm hungry, I wake up thinking of fresh butter, of thick cream, of coffee, of ham… and after breakfast I think about lunch, I think about… what comes after lunch, the thing that sets this hunger aflame, all these hungers which I now experience, which are so intense…!'

She let the hands which had been digging into her waist and at her throat fall back, called over to me in the same recriminatory tone: 'Could I have predicted, me, honestly…'

Her voice changed: 'My God, he says I make him so happy…'

I couldn't stop myself, I enlaced my arms round her neck: 'Marco, don't think about so many things all at once! What you've said just now answers everything, explains everything, makes everything else immaterial! Be happy, Marco, make him happy, send the rest packing!'

We embraced. She left, serene and reassured, comfortably

buoyed on her newly broadened hips. It was the time of year when we made our annual Bayreuth trip, M. Willy and I, and I made sure to send Marco lots of Wagnerian postcards decorated with musical leitmotifs. As soon as I got back, I arranged to meet Marco in our teashop. She had not become any thinner, or younger either. As others acquire stooping backs or increasing girth, she was developing a positively shelf-like bosom.

'And you haven't been away from Paris at all, Marco? Nothing has changed?'

'Nothing, thank goodness.'

She touched the wooden table top to ward off ill-luck. For want of any further details, I took her gesture to mean that Marco still belonged, body and soul, to Lieutenant Trallard. No less eloquent an indication, the only questions Marco asked about my stay in Bayreuth were pure politenesses—and I suspected she hardly listened to my replies even then.

She blushed when I asked her in my turn: 'And work, Marco? Serials on the drawing board for next season?'

'Oh! Not really…' she said, sounding bored. 'A publishing house wants a novel for children, eight to fourteen… as if I had any idea how to go about that! Besides…'

A soft and animal-like expression passed like a cloud over her face.

'Besides, I feel so lazy… so very lazy…!'

When Masson, hearing we were back, came to jab three times on our bell, he quickly told me he knew "everything", from Marco's own lips. To my surprise, he spoke about Lieutenant Trallard positively. He did not dismiss him as a tenth-rate gigolo, nor as an alcoholic heading for premature baldness, nor as a garrison-town dandy. On the other hand, I found him quite hard on Marco, and more cold than hard.

'No, come on, Paul, what is there in this whole business you can blame Marco for?'

'Well, pooh… nothing,' Paul Masson said.

'And they're madly happy together, you know!'

'Madly is no exaggeration, it seems to me.'

He gave a thin laugh, copied by M. Willy. Nasty laughter, which mocked both Marco and me, and which was accompanied by judgemental and tactless remarks, dire prognostications expressed with total certainty and indifference, as if the adventure which was illuminating Marco's autumn years was nothing more than a minor filler in yesterday's newspaper.

'In physical terms,' Paul Masson would say, 'Marco in fact *had* reached the stage known as a "brewer's mare". When a gazelle has turned into a broad-bottomed brood mare, things don't look good for her. Lieutenant Trallard *has* behaved perfectly correctly. It's Marco who has compromised Lieutenant Trallard.'

'Compromised? You're mad, Masson! You make assertions, honestly…'

'Little lady, a child of three would tell you the same as me, that the foremost, the urgent duty of Marco was to remain thin, charming, a twilight creature, furtive, damp with rain, not to burst out into blooming health, not to frighten the crowd by shouting: "Yes, that's it! That's it! I…"'

'Masson!'

I grew indignant, I whipped Masson with my rope of hair. I found it impossible to understand a bizarre and exclusively male sort of severity, directed at an exclusively female innocence. The judgements that passed between the two men, who dismissed from "the Marco case" any extenuating circumstances, I listened to as if I was hearing a lesson in higher mathematics…

'She *was not* suitable for it,' one of them would decree. 'To be, at the age of forty-six, the mistress of a man of twenty-five, she regarded as an amusing adventure.'

'Whereas it is a full-time occupation,' the other would say.

'A sport, rather.'

'No. A sport is an occupation without benefits. But she's not even going to realise that a break-up, for her, is the best that can be hoped for…'

I had not yet become insensitive to the mixture of affected cynicism, literary paradoxes, which around 1900 kept cultivated, bitter and futureless men high in their own esteem.

September had come to Paris, with its fine dry weather, its red evening skies. I was cross with the town and with the marital decisions that had shortened my holidays. One day I received a note which I stared at in surprise, for I was not familiar with Marco's writing, a regular enough hand but one whose separately spaced letters nevertheless betrayed an agitation of the heart. She wanted to speak to me. I waited for her at the hour when, with the setting of the sun, the redness in the sky sent a disturbing wine-coloured glow through the yellow-curtained window panes. I was pleased to see her bearing no trace of any kind of disorder. As if there were only one possible topic of conversation, Marco said straightaway: 'What do you think, Alex is being sent on a mission.'

'A mission? Where to?'

'Morocco.'

'When?'

'At any moment. In a week or so. Appointed by the Minister for War.'

'And… is it inevitable?'

'His father, General Trallard… yes, his father, if he were to intervene personally, he might… but he views this mission—which is far from being without danger—as a great favour… so…'

Her hand sketched out a little gesture, but fell back into her lap, leaving it unfinished, and she relapsed into silence and stared vaguely into the distance. Her heavy shoulders, her full and pale cheeks and her beautiful tragic eyes lent her the air of a queen of the stage.

'Is it a long thing, Marco, a mission?'

'I don't know, I've no idea. He's talking about three, four months, maybe five…'

'Well, Marco,' I said cheerfully, 'what's three or four months? You'll just wait for him, that's all.'

She didn't appear to hear me. She seemed to be studying with great concentration a mark the cleaner had written inside her glove in violet ink.

'Marco,' I risked saying, 'can't you accompany him there, live somewhere nearby?'

And I at once regretted having spoken.

Marco, packing trunks, dresses—Marco as a European mistress, or Marco as a native wife, silver bangles, couscous, fringed scarves. The pictures my imagination flashed at me made me afraid—afraid for Marco…

'Of course,' I hastily added, 'it's not practical…'

Night was coming, and I got up to bring us some lights, but Marco held me back.

'Wait,' she said. 'There's something else. I'd prefer not to speak to you about it here. Will you come round tomorrow, to my flat? I have some good China tea, some savoury cakes from boulevard Malesherbes…'

'I'd love to, Marco! But…'

'I'm not expecting anyone tomorrow. Come, there's something you can help me with. Don't light the lamps, the light in the hall is good enough for me.'

*

Marco's little "furnished rooms" had also changed. An arrangement of curtains on a wooden frame, behind the entrance door, made for the semblance of a hallway. The brass bed had become a divan, and a few new pieces of furniture seemed to me very decent, as well as some oriental carpets. A Venetian mirror with rosettes, over the mantelpiece, reflected red and white dahlias. In the perfume that scented the room I recognised Marco's, married, if I may put it so, to another, spicier fragrance. The second and smaller room served as a bathroom, I glimpsed a white tub, a shower attachment close to the ceiling. As I entered I said something like: 'You've made it very nice, Marco.'

A disturbed September, much too cold for the time of year, made no impression in this compact dwelling, whose thick walls and closed windows accounted for the stillness of the air. Marco was already busying herself with tea, laying out our two cups, our two plates. 'She's not expecting anyone,' I was thinking. She offered me greengages heaped on a saucer, warmed the teapot.

'You have such pretty little hands, Marco!'

She clattered a cup suddenly, as if the least unwonted sound might risk upsetting the measured carefulness of her movements. We consumed this sketchy meal, which disguises and delays the embarrassment of explanations, ruptures, silences, and we nevertheless came to the moment when Marco was obliged to speak to me. And it was high time, I could see her resolution crumbling. We are led to think it strange, if not comical, that a chubby person should give signs of being at the end of her tether, and I was amazed that Marco could be simultaneously so ample and so hesitant. She took herself in hand: I saw her face regain its belligerent aristocratic look. The cigarette she hungrily lit after tea completed her recovery. A flash of henna in her short hair enhanced the effect.

'Well,' she said in a clear voice, 'I think it's all over.'

It seemed certain she had not prepared for her opening remark to employ such a striking word, for she stopped, as if stupefied.

'Over? What do you mean, over?'

'You know very well what I mean,' she said. 'If, as I believe, you love me a little, you will try to help me, but… in any case, I'm going to tell you…'

Those were more or less the last considered words she spoke. From the tale that followed I am obliged to extract the elements that made it, on Marco's lips, so confused and so terribly clear.

She explained the way many women explain, going far and futilely back into the past, a past which was her sole and dazzling adventure in love. She continually repeated herself, corrected dates: 'So it was on a Thursday, the twenty-sixth of

December… what am I saying? A Friday, since we'd been to Prunier's* for a fasting dinner… he's a practising catholic, and fasts on Fridays…'

Then the minutiae of her account became unravelled, scattered to the winds. Marco rambled, her sentences a muddle of half-formed expressions, saying, 'No, I'll pass over that', 'Ah, là, là, I'm getting all mixed up', and constantly repeating 'You see what I mean'. Grief's power of gesticulation had her slapping her knees with the flat of her hand, flinging her head back against the tall wings of her armchair…

All the while, for as long as she could not stem the rush of words and the banality that give all such accounts of amorous disasters a cosy, domestic feel, for as long as she mingled with some fairly crass circumlocutions the unappealing mime of lowering her eyelashes and turning her head aside, my interest was cool, I wanted to leave, I even had to clench my jaws to suppress a reflex yawn. I found Marco altogether too commonplace as a woman in love, and also thought she was taking an inordinate time to explain how so much praise for a handsome young soldier could end in disaster, a wholly exceptional one, as all disasters are.

'And then one day…' Marco said at last.

She placed her elbows on the arms of the chair. I imitated her and we leant towards each other. Marco emerged from her meandering lamentations and I saw in her soft and pleading eyes a watchful gleam, a look that was not to be deceived. Her tone of voice changed also, and I attempt here to summarise the dramatic part of her tale.

She had not forgotten to mention, in her initial flood of words, the "mad passion of their embraces", the splendid vigour with which the young man, aflame with desire, pushed through the half-open street door, flung back the door to her room, and from there leapt in a single bound to the divan where Marco was waiting for him, recumbent. He would tolerate no diversions, no discussions. Impetuosity has its rites. Marco gave me to understand that lieutenant, gloves and képi, tumbled in disorder, more often than not, straight on to the divan. Poetry, sweet nothings, only came afterwards. At this point in her account, Marco interrupted herself, with a measure of pride, and directed her gaze towards a photograph frame, nickel and bevelled glass. Her silence and her glance invited me to all manner of conjectures, and perhaps to feelings of envy.

'So then one day…' Marco said.

A day of special splendour, obviously. One of those days when the Paris rain, some unknown dampness that mists the mirrors, some unknown need to cast off clothes, induce lovers to shut out the world and turn day into night, 'one of those days,' said Marco, 'which are the ruination of both body and soul…' I had no choice but to follow my friend and to imagine her—she forced me—half naked, on the divan, recovering from one of those ecstatic encounters, so physical and so rough that she called them "evil spells"… it was at that moment that her hand, straying over the bed, came up against the képi, and that she yielded to one of the most feminine of reflexes: she sat up in her rumpled chemise, planted the képi at a jaunty angle, gave it a roguish tap, and broke into song:

'Drums, trumpets, the band at their head,
See them come, the regiment…'

'I have never seen,' Marco told me, 'never seen Alex's expression change like that. An expression… impossible to read. An expression I would call horrific, if he weren't so handsome… I can't tell you what I felt…'

She paused, looked over to the empty divan bed.

'And then, Marco, what did he say to you?'

'Why, nothing, I took the képi off, I adjusted my clothing, got out of bed, we made tea… in short, everything was just as normal. But since that day I've caught Alex, once or twice, with that same look on his face, and such a strange expression in his eyes… I can't move away from the idea that that képi has been fatal for me. Has it brought back a bad memory? I wanted your impression. Tell me, don't try to be tactful, tell me what you really think.'

I was careful to compose my features before replying, so fearful was I that they might resemble Lieutenant Trallard's, from consternation, disapproval and shock. Oh, Marco! In a single moment I lost you, I wept for you;—I saw you. I saw you as Alexis Trallard had seen you. I felt his contempt for the outsized breasts, the shoulders slipping from the violently disarranged chemise. And the grainy skin of the neck, scored with lines, and the red patches of skin under the ears, the chin abandoned to its own devices, beyond remedy… and the lower eyelid that sags and folds like a dried-up stream after love, and the drunken flame that fails to fade swiftly enough from the overripe features it has swamped… on top of all that, the képi! The képi, its rigid top, its perky visor, tipped over the mischievously winking eye:

"*Drums, trumpets, band at their head…*"

'I know very well,' Marco continued, 'that between lovers it only takes a trifle to ruin a highly-charged atmosphere… I know very well…'

Alas, what did she know?

'And after that, Marco? How did it end?'

'End? But I'm telling you. Nothing else has happened. The Morocco mission has come up. Its date has been brought forward twice. But that's not the only reason why I've been feeling so uneasy. There have been other things, signs…'

'What signs?'

She did not dare to be more specific. She brushed away my question with her hand, turned her head away.

'Oh, nothing…! Some… some differences…'

She cocked an ear towards the door.

'I haven't seen him for three days,' she said. 'Obviously he has to make preparations for this mission… but…'

She smiled to herself.

'But I am not a child,' she said, her tone quite detached. 'Besides, he writes to me. Little notes by telegram.'

'What are these notes like?'

'Oh, charming! Of course, they're charming. He may be very young, but he's not completely a child either.'

As I had stood up, Marco suddenly became full of anguish, humble, took my hands: 'What do you think I ought to do? What does one do, in cases like this?'

'How should I know, Marco? I think there's nothing to do but wait… I think that whatever else, there's the question of your dignity…'

She gave an unexpected peal of laughter: 'My dignity! Oh, you do make me laugh! My dignity! Oh, these young women…'

Her laughter and the way she looked at me I found intolerable.

'But Marco, you ask me for advice, I tell you what my hearts says…'

She continued to laugh, shrugging her shoulders. Still laughing, she casually opened the door for me. I thought she was going to embrace me, that we would arrange our next meeting, but I was hardly outside before she shut her door again without having said another word to me except: 'My dignity! Ah, no, it's too comical!'

*

If I am sticking to the facts, this is the end of Marco's story. Marco had a lover for a while, Marco no longer had a lover. Marco had "laid a hand on the axe", that is to say, had donned the fatal képi, and at the worst possible moment… at the moment when a man is a sad harp still quivering, an explorer returned from a country he has glimpsed but not reached, a lucid penitent, one who swears "I will not do this again" and falls to his knees begging absolution…

I was stubborn enough to insist on seeing Marco again, after some days had passed. I rang and knocked at her door, which did not open. I went back again, for I could sense Marco there, alone, grown hard and feverish, behind the barrier she had erected. My mouth to the door crack, I said 'It's me', and Marco let me in. Immediately I saw that she regretted opening the door. With a distracted air, she was smoothing the loose skin of her small hands so that it rode up towards her wrists, like the cuffs of a glove. I refused to be intimidated and I said I wanted, I demanded, she come to dinner that very evening at my house. And I exercised my authority by adding: 'I suppose Lieutenant Trallard has gone?'

'Yes,' Marco said.

'How long will it take him to get there?'

'He isn't *there*,' said Marco. 'He's at Ville-d'Avray,* at his father's place. It amounts to the same thing.'

'Ah,' I said, after which I didn't know what else to say.

'In point of fact,' Marco continued, 'why shouldn't I come and have dinner with you?'

I exclaimed, I thanked her, I leapt round her in joy, like some little fox terrier. I doubt that she was much deceived. When I had her sitting in my own apartment, in the warmth, lit by my lamp, I was able to measure not just Marco's decline, but a strange sort of reduction. Diminished in size —she was getting thinner—diminished in tone—she spoke in a clipped little voice. She must have been forgetting to eat and finding it hard to sleep.

Masson came after dinner, met Marco with as much apprehension as his inscrutable features were able to express. He greeted her in a sideways sort of fashion, like a crab.

'Look, it's Masson,' Marco said, indifferent. 'Good evening, Paul.'

They engaged in conversation like old friends, in other words a conversation devoid of interest. I listened to them and thought that such a flow of commonplaces must be relaxing for Marco. She left early and we remained alone, Masson and I.

'Don't you think she looks out of sorts, eh, Paul, our poor Marco…?'

'Yes,' Masson said. 'It's the priest phase.'

'The what phase?'

'The priest. When a woman, who's up to then been a very feminine woman, begins to look like a priest, it's a sign she no longer has any hopes of the other sex, neither kindnesses nor cruelties. A certain yellowish pallor, a sad nose, a tight-lipped smile, drooping jowls: there you have Marco. The priest, I'm telling you, the priest.'

He rose to leave, and added: 'Just between us two, I prefer this for her than the odalisque phase.'

I made a point thereafter of not neglecting Marco. She rapidly grew thinner. It is difficult to hold in check a person who is melting away, I should have written: who is shrinking back into herself. She moved, that is to say she packed her trunk and took it off to some other small furnished room. I saw her frequently, and never did she mention Lieutenant Trallard. Then I saw her less often, and the failure of will came much more from her side than from mine. She seemed, strangely, to be setting herself the task of turning into a frail little old woman. Time passed…

'But, Masson, what's happening with Marco? It's been ages… do you have any news of Marco yourself?'

'Yes,' said Masson.

'And you haven't said anything!'

'You haven't asked me!'

'Quick, where is she?'

'In the *Bibliothèque Nationale* almost every day. She's been translating, from English, an extraordinary report from

Bangui in the French Congo. Since the manuscript is a bit short to make a full volume, she's filling it out at the publisher's request, and she's doing her research at the *Bibliothèque*.'

'So she's taken up the same old way of life,' I said pensively, 'the one she led before Lieutenant Trallard.'

'Oh, no!' Masson said. 'There's been a significant change in her life!'

'What's that? Come on, do I have to drag everything out of you?'

'Now,' said Masson, 'Marco is getting two *sous* a line.'

THE BUDDING SHOOT

'But you have no reason to stay in Paris,' I was saying, in May 1940, to my old friend—what shall I call him? Let's say Chaveriat, yes, Albin Chaveriat; there are quite a lot of Chaveriats in France, originally from the Basque country, many now rooted in Franche-Comté and more or less everywhere, enough for no particular one of them to object to my making use of the name—'you will only languish in Paris for as long as this war lasts: go and settle for a while in the country. Why not meet up with Curnonsky* again at Riec-sur-Belon, at Mélanie's place?'

'I don't like the wind on the coast,' said Chaveriat. 'And I don't want to eat too well either. I would lose my waist.'

'The South? Saint-Tropez? Cavalaire?'

Chaveriat's short white moustache bristled.

'Tarted up like fairgrounds… carnivals for the dead,

too sinister.'

'Do you see yourself more as a paying guest? Go to Normandy, stay with the Hersents, who won't be shifting from their estate unless someone drives them out with fire and brimstone. There's a river, a billiard room, a tennis court—badly maintained—a croquet lawn… the whole family is very healthy, and just with their daughters and nieces there's no shortage of young women…'

'Not a word more. You've just said the one thing that's sure to keep me away.'

'So nothing attracts you, not fresh breezes, not cheapness, not the South, not young women… you are a difficult man to pigeon-hole, Albin.'

'I always have been, dear friend. It is what has made me, in the end, the pearl among bachelors…'

Chaveriat walked, without his stick, to one of my three windows. When he concentrated, he hardly limped. Last year, "a clot in the heart", as they used to call it, set him back, before a more lasting disability humbled his imposing bearing as a man still slim at sixty-eight. With his cropped white hair, his dark and lively eye, moustache clipped with scissors, it was said of him that he must, in his younger days, have made many women despair. But I can confirm that back in 1906 he was no more than a fairly ordinary brown-haired fellow.

A good walker, he loved country rambles as much as hairdressers love a day on the river bank, fishing. Out in the countryside, Albin, who did not hunt, would go for long walks with a gun. He would bring back, instead of game, a small peach sapling knocked flat by a squall of hail, an abandoned cat, a handkerchief full of *ceps*. Such traits made him very likeable. In vain, and at long intervals, I tried to discover the one thing missing from our friendship, limited as it was by secrecy, well-guarded, concerning the love life of Albin Chaveriat. Before his death, he only revealed one such secret, on that same day that I suggested he get through the war—we did not know, in May 1940, quite what those words would mean—in a place brightened by the presence of young women. For I pressed him on his refusal, which he had made with the reticence and reserve that prompt the other party to make the inevitable response: 'You will not leave my house, my fine fellow, until you have told me the whole story!'

Albin did not leave my house. It was all the easier to persuade him to stay because we had for dinner some excellent fish, very fresh, mushrooms removed from the heat before they could be reduced to tasteless scraps, as happens when served at almost every table in France, and a semi-liquid chocolate cream, to satisfy both those who like to eat it with a spoon and those who prefer to drink it straight from the little pot… in 1940, our Paris markets were still so rich in produce that we would wander through the Les Halles district simply for the pleasure of feasting our eyes. We had adopted a language which included expressions like "funny sort of war", "phoney war", and we were, all of us, unable to sense what was in the wind, a little like beasts with no sense of smell…

To loosen his discreet tongue, I offered my fellow-diner, the remains of my good *marc*.

'Is it the Hersents who put you off Normandy, colonel, or their abundance of young women?'

Chaveriat hadn't laughed for a long time when someone called him that. I think he used to quite like it when we acknowledged with this fantasy rank his white hair *en brosse*, his moustache and his eminently excusable limp.

'Neither one nor the other, dear friend. Nowhere charms me as much as Normandy, and I've always enjoyed the company of young women, or rather a young girl.'

'Gracious!'

'Does that surprise you? Why? We've only known each other for twenty-five years, and I'm sixty-eight. Do you imagine that for nearly forty years I did nothing more than measure up to the image you've formed of me and which is doubtless very different from the image I have of myself? Yes, the two things I liked above all else were young women and hunting. Now, I wouldn't point a gun at a jay; and one young girl not so much cured me as drove me away from young girls… you want a story, you are going to get it. It is not pretty, far from it. But it can no longer do any harm to anyone, and by now its heroine has, though I fear it for her sake, sons of eighteen.

Where did the taste for young girls come from? I believe it was through a male friendship. Between fifteen and twenty, I had a friend, one of those companions of adolescence to whom a normal boy is more faithful in his heart than to a mistress. Once past twenty, various things, a woman, military service, a profession burst in on one's life and spoil that beautiful idyll of mutual support. Even military service made little difference to Eyrand and me, we did it together. The first betrayal came from him, I use the word to describe his marriage. To marry at twenty-three-and-a-half, my family declared it an "imprudence". As for me, I have just told you what I called our separation. No, thank you, one glass of *marc* is enough. If I drank more, I would tell the story badly and without the necessary impartiality.

I remember that I flatly refused to go and spend the holidays with Eyrand, during the first year of his marriage, in a small manor house which represented, with its thirty or so hectares, the most visible part of his wife's dowry, and which he worked on himself. He wrote to me again, without success, he sent me snaps picturing his young wife, his beef cattle, his small farm-holding, but I remained in a sulk, I sent back mindless letters in response because I thought his wife would read them… and also because my friend's letters had nothing to express but a blinkered content. Never a doubt, never a moment's trouble, never a worry or anything at all I could have consoled him for… in fact, I will have a drop of *marc*. A drop, no higher up than the star cut in the glass…

In the end Eyrand grew tired, as you may imagine. When I saw I had lost, largely through my own fault, a friend I never could ever dream of replacing, I made myself sociable only to creatures of the female kind, very young ones, in whom I could appreciate an abrupt sincerity of manner, a show of interest—virtually always affected—, an outline of beauty to come, a character still in development. They were seventeen, eighteen, a little more, a little less, while I was closing in on thirty, and at their side I believed I was the same age as they were. At their side… I can say more accurately and truthfully, in their arms. What accomplishments does a girl have at that age that are ready to be used, that she can be enthusiastic about, apart from sensuality…? No, let's not argue about it, I know you don't share my opinion. You will not prevent me, and for good reasons, from having nurtured an almost horrified preference for that brew of passion, abruptness, extravagance and caution, all co-existing in a girl who has, how to put it… who has passed a certain watershed. You have to have known a fair number of young girls to appreciate that, compared with fully-developed women, most of them are extraordinary risk-takers, the inspired of their kind, and that in dangerous unions nothing can match them for serenity. Public opinion has its formula: "Only a coward attacks young girls…" Lord! I can tell you that on the contrary one needs a very particular sort of temperament, and a rare self-control to resist them. And one basic thing, get out of your head the idea that my taste ever developed into a monomania, perversely excluding anything else. In matters of love, I have often been a man like any other, involved for a time in a relationship, drawn towards a sensible marriage, then running away from it no less sensibly, unable to commit—I'm saying, a man like all the other men.

In 1923, I no longer hunted, but I accepted invitations to hunting parties. One of my friends, a pharmacist, now retired from business—there have been parts of France where all the big estates, at one time, passed into the hands of these former pharmacists—this friend had bought a property in the Doubs that was so handsome, I arranged my whole year with a view to an autumn vacation, between the 15th August and the 15th October. I was less pleased with life there than I had hoped, thanks to a badly matched set of guests and the lavish gluttony that was the rule. Food and drink, everything was to excess, and every single day. To the point where I adopted the guise of a dreamer with a bad liver, to have the right to solitude and sobriety. The local bigwigs tapped me on the shoulder after meals, belching discreetly: "What's this, can't take it? You ought to see someone..." I refrained from replying that on the contrary I would have preferred to see no one at all, and made myself scarce. Unless I took on the task of instructing a reasonably good-looking woman, a cousin of the pharmaceutical lord of the manor, in how to draw up the catalogue for a library, and other agreeable occupations for the warmer times of day.

What a marvellous part of the country that Doubs region is, dear friend! And what a fine property! The new squire hadn't had time to embellish it to any disastrous degree, nor to change its fundamental character which, up in those hills in September, is not parched but still extremely hot. The days, though shorter, remained torrid, enough to burn your hands when you dined out of doors, and at night a wonderful chill came through the windows just before dawn. It turned the leaves on the cherry trees bright red, and those on the chestnuts and elms a precocious yellow. There never was a more yellow season, and that includes the grass in the fields, which had received no rain and failed to produce the second hay crop. But because of the density of the coppices, the undergrowth still retained its moisture, and you could find all sorts of mushrooms. There are a lot of "violets" in the Franche-Comté. The violet is a sort of delicate mushroom.

Sparrowhawks, they too a golden yellow, escorted me part of the way, circling high above my head to see what I was going to do, and as I was innocent of any design, they wheeled away.

Being a good walker (I'm speaking of twenty years ago), I went up hill and down dale; I discovered a little system of locks in the park, the gates rotting, the pool dried up, the remains of a sculpture, a saint in its niche, at one time a viewpoint. Nothing had been visible from it for a long time, infested as it was with rabbit droppings and prickly butcher's broom. I walked out of the park without realising because the pharmacist preferred installing bathrooms everywhere rather than having his boundary walls rebuilt. But five hundred metres further on the land grew more organised, divided into small, cultivated plots bounded by low dry-stone walls, which made nice warm retreats for adders. Despite all the hillocks, the somewhat densely packed crests and valleys of the country, I didn't lose my way. I never wander off course, you know. What are you smiling at? All right, I understand. No, thank you, no more *marc*. A glass of cold water would be perfect.

Perhaps you are thinking I'm making too much of the countryside. But the fact is, that long-ago autumn has left such a sun-scorched impression on me… on certain mornings, the dew looked like a layer of white frost, and then one roasted until the evening, and remained like that even then, and the grapes—a small black variety, the bunches so tight an ant couldn't have crawled in—ripened early on the walls of the farm, on the gatekeepers' lodges, at the same time as the blue and mauve scabious confirmed that this fiery summer would soon have to be called autumn. I was content, content with no need for words, with hardly a thought in my head; I let my skin tan brown, I fancied I had the agreeable appearance of a country gentleman. One day… yes, you see, I'm getting there.

One day, I was out beyond the estate. I had left behind all the worshippers of fine weather. I was on a hillside in the woods, I was climbing the steepish slope of a forest track, grassy but bearing the marks of wheels. I was walking between lines of birches whose golden leaves the wind was already dislodging, tiny, light leaves which fluttered for ages before coming to earth. Towards the top of the slope I noticed that the birches gave way to apple trees, bordering a meadow. Behind the apples, a handsome stand of pines, slightly gloomy-looking, more than half obscured an ancient building, a house, with a gable of old tiles, very prettily set sideways, as if carefully planned, at the top of the slope. A great cloak of Virginia creeper, pink in places, covered one shoulder. A kitchen garden to one side, the main garden overgrown with greenery, a drive which shimmered in the heat haze with the purplish-blue of the Franche-Comté… I thought: "How pretty, how neglected…" and I heard a murmur of water, besides. Free-flowing water is a rare blessing in these little mountains… on the other side of the low and crumbling wall, the horned forehead of a goat touched my hand, a pair of narrow oval pupils stared at me. I reached my hand out to scratch the pretty black forehead, marked with a star. It did not turn away.

'Don't touch her, don't touch her, she'll charge you!' a young voice cried.

The accent in those parts drags on the vowels, as you know. '*Doan't* touch 'er! She'll *chaarge* you!' Naturally, I put my hand out, and in a bound the goat was after me, pretty as a devil, pursued by a child shouting: '*Baad* animal, wait!' A child… no. Girls of fifteen or so are not what I call children. I'd lose too many. The young woman seized the goat by the horns and turned it deftly on its side. The goat got up and bounded away, taking little leaps with all four feet.

'It's cross,' the girl said.

She regained her breath, panting with mouth half open. A blonde, a bit deeper than blonde perhaps, on the edge of red, freckles on her cheeks and forehead, lashes the colour of fire. But nothing like those albino redheads, on the contrary an extraordinarily healthy complexion under the scattering of freckles, and like the cheeks, speckles in the eyes too, little brown flecks on a grey-green iris. One of the first features I noticed was the colour of the wispy hair at her temples and the nape of her neck (pretentiously, she wore her hair in a chignon). It curled, almost pink, shot through by the midday sun. For it was noon, a noon to peel your nose, on the summit of this bare hilltop.

I said to her: 'You have done nothing less than save my life, *mademoiselle.*'

She laughed, moving her shoulders like a coquettish girl untutored in good manners. The inside of her mouth, as she raised her chin to laugh, was on view right to her molars, and I think she threw her head back on purpose. It's always a rare thing, a faultless set of teeth, in country girls. Country girls… my young woman was not wearing an apron, and she was dressed carelessly rather than rustically. A ready-made blouse, blue with white spots, a badly cut skirt and a leather belt—that was the outer look. Underneath, there was a young creature… the word fulsome, so rarely heard nowadays, describes a type of beauty which, believe me, is genuinely intoxicating when the beauty is adolescent. While I made the little thing laugh with facile jokes, I was thinking, confronted with this precocious bounty, this involuntary provocation, I was thinking of the drawings Boucher* made of Louise O'Morphy,* who had no sooner finished growing than her whole plump body proclaimed its urgent mission and was crying out to lovers: "Deliver me from myself, or I shall burst!"

My little O'Morphy of the Franche-Comté blushed after a while, but only because she remembered she had strung round her neck, as all children do every autumn, a necklace of "square bonnets", you know, those bright pink berries, with their four-lobed flowerheads, from a wild spindle tree… I'm silly, as obviously you know. She furiously broke the necklace and I told her: 'That was a shame, it suited you so well. May I know the name of my protectress?'

'Louisette… Louise,' she corrected herself with a show of dignity.

I replied that I was called Albin, and with a little twitch of the mouth she indicated that it was fine with her. She examined me stealthily, putting a hand over her eyes as if to shield herself from the sun. A voice called her, and she answered with a loud and shrill "yes".

'I live here,' she said, before leaving me. 'There, in the château.'

She named her home, with an affected pride. Then she began to run back to her "château" with long boyish strides.

I don't imagine you'll be surprised when I tell you that… no, not the next day. The day after that, I braved the morning sun of half past eleven, at the same spot. The previous day, I had taken advantage of a motor car that was going shopping to ride into town and buy a little necklace made from coral, just about the same colour as the bright pink flowers… I'm sorry, what did you say, dear friend? That was a wicked thing to do, and classic? Allow me to defend myself. The lover of young girls is neither so simple nor so firmly resolved as to imagine his intentions already fulfilled when he hasn't even had time to work out what they are. But I recognise that his way of acting is all too often redolent of the cheap and fateful methods Faust was instructed in by a demon uninspired in stratagems. The jesting pleasantries of lord to peasant girl… I took up position, then, at the margin of the wood, in the same burning heat that seemed unlikely ever to end, in that same unforgiving light of eleven o'clock, which ripened, before their time, apples, blackberries, and those bush peaches that are known, for good reason, as stone fruit. And there I saw no Louisette, but I heard the free-flowing water, whose path was marked on the other side of the hill by a line of greener bushes, some alders and a few willows. I had been walking fast, I was dying to go over and drink. Suddenly my young girl was there, three strides away, with no sound of footsteps or rustling of branches. She looked at me with a stare so intense I could only translate its meaning as akin to a series of short exclamations, like: "Well! Is that you? What do you want? I'm waiting. Speak. Do something!" I took care not to employ that sort of language myself, and I greeted her politely, as would any man have done, animated or not by evil designs.

'Good day, *mademoiselle* Louisette.'

She held out her hand like a young girl who has no idea how to shake hands, an impersonal little paw.

'Good day, *monsieur*.'

'I've brought you back the necklace you broke the other day…'

And I offered my little necklace, unwrapped and as it was. Louisette reacted with a twitch of the neck, and its rippling motion made me shiver with delight. A column of flesh so exactly, evenly filled, a roundness that betrayed nothing of its inner structure, I have never seen anything quite the same, carried to an extraordinary degree of succulence, I have never seen anything quite like that in anyone but her… and then, I was not dealing with some bronzed girl off the beaches. Except for the triumphant colouring of the face and a small, tanned triangle in the opening of the blouse, the colour of her body began immediately at the base of the neck, such a pale colour, barely even pink…

…like a lily under purple skies…

Oh, you can laugh. Plenty of times I have felt poetry rise inside me, above any physical feeling. Poetry has often, in similar circumstances, saved a young girl, and me, from myself…

So I offered my necklace, fastened with a little gold clasp. But Louisette refused it with a toss of the head.

'No,' she added.

'You don't want it? You find it ugly?'

'No. But I can't take it.'

'It's an object of no value,' I said foolishly.

'That doesn't matter. I can't take it because of *maman*. What would *maman* say if she saw me with a necklace?'

'Could you… have found it?'

She gave a disillusioned smile. Her brown-flecked eyes were still on mine. Spots of sunlight danced from her golden eyelashes to her chin. I have never seen a complexion quite like hers, such a lightly sculpted mouth, such delicately flared nostrils… what…? Was she pretty? True, I haven't told you if she was pretty. I don't think she was particularly pretty, in fact. Not well-presented, in any case. Her shining hair I could see was held in place by ugly hairpins of tarnished metal. I could see her stockings, of beige linen or cotton, were not very clean. I have an unfailing eye for some things…

She was looking at me so… what shall I say?… so brazenly that I became anxious about my own appearance for a moment, just for a moment. The clothes I was wearing were so plain and simple they couldn't possibly reflect badly on me: a soft-collared shirt, trousers in a tough material to ward off brambles, jacket over my arm… and I was nineteen years younger than I am today. Before it became the fashion, I went about bareheaded, protected by my thick thatch of hair, turned white already, alas! And physically rake-like, as you have always known me.

Naturally, I looked back at Louisette, but more cautiously, let's say in a more civilised manner. But nevertheless I saw that she had elongated the outer corners of her eyelids by means of two small pencil strokes. Such a preposterous piece of coquetry, so silly, made me laugh out loud. It was like when you see children celebrating Shrove Tuesday gravely sporting horsehair beards.

You may well imagine my young girl was not pleased. She understood only too well and put her two forefingers to the corners of her eyes. I took advantage of her discomfiture to establish some authority.

'This is a fine thing,' I told her. 'At your age? You refuse a bauble from me for fear of your mother, yet you're not afraid to make your eyes up?'

She turned her shoulders away, in a movement familiar to all girls who haven't been brought up properly. But no girl, badly brought up or not, moved shoulders quite like hers inside her blouse, nor the youthful pair of breasts that moved with them. I hoped she might shed a tear or two, and that I could console her.

'Take this little necklace,' I told her, 'or I'll throw it away.'

'Throw it away,' she said promptly. 'I certainly won't pick it up. You'd better give it to another girl.'

'Are you so afraid of your mother?'

She shook her head in denial again before speaking.

'No. I'm afraid of her bad opinion.'

'And your father, is he the rigorous sort?'

'Is he what?'

'Is he strict with you?'

'No. He's dead.'

'I'm sorry… was he old?'

'Fifty-two.'

That was, to within a few months, my own age, and I automatically stood up straighter.

'So, you live alone with your mother?'

'And the Biguets who come to share the harvesting.'

'That water I can hear flowing, is that yours?'

'Yes. It's the spring.'

'A spring! And a big enough one to hear it from here… that's worth a fortune!'

'It's the best,' said Louisette simply.

Her expression changed, she cast a wrathful glance in my direction.

'You're not another of those people who *waant* to buy it *fraam* us?'

Who *waant* to buy it *fraam* us… I did not find her accent, strong on certain words, at all displeasing. On the contrary.

I reassured her: 'No, no, Louisette! I'm on holiday at ***... staying with the new owner. I don't want to take your stream from you... but I think I could drink the whole thing up, I'm so thirsty.'

She spread her hands in a sign of regret and helplessness: 'Not that, I can't take you in and let you drink from it. My mother'd find it very funny if I was talking to someone she doesn't know. Unless we go round the outside...'

'The outside, where's the outside?'

With a wink, a lift of the eyebrows, a pursing of the lips, she sent me a message of complicity beyond anything I'd hoped for, and which delighted me. I saw her destined for a life of dissimulation, forbidden connivance and ultimately sin. As best I could, I replied in similar fashion, and we started back again, the girl leading, me following behind, down the shaded track at the edge of the wood, along the low and crumbling wall that the goat had jumped over to *chaarge* me.

'Where is my enemy the goat, *mademoiselle* Louisette?'

'In the fields. We've three goats, but she's got the nicest nature.'

Louisette answered me without turning her head, and I was happy enough to study at my leisure the nape of her neck, revealed by her hair, pinned high in its chignon, the small ears, warmly pink, the flat, symmetrical shoulder blades, and the slight, elastic swell of the hips below the tightly fastened leather belt... as I said, a work with no angles or awkward edges, and moreover with no nobility other than its state of precocious perfection... a young creature so obviously made for one specific purpose, an imbecile would have thought it cynical. But I am not an imbecile, dear friend. I need to assert the fact, since I have to introduce you very shortly to a Chaveriat hitherto unknown, and one who was for a long time determined to remain so. For I was never a man to flaunt my vices, if indeed there is any vice in them.

So I walked behind this little thing, admiring her. I was trying to come up with an expression that defined her, a classification, informed by her native effrontery, her willingness to serve my curiosity, to deceive the watchful mother. Already, I was calling her "The prettiest little maid in France". Everyone can make a mistake.

Where the crumbling wall made an elbow bend, we left the shelter of the trees. The track was now no more than a footpath, descending quite steeply, and the wall became taller in equal measure, hiding from us the "château". An old wall, bursting with blooms like a flowerbed. The scabious, the last foxgloves, some valerians, which I have always noticed as being very red in the Franche-Comté, and some bignonia somewhat overwhelmed by the ivy…

'What a beautiful wall!' I said to Louisette.

She only answered with a nod, and I thought she preferred not to allow her voice to be heard in conversation with a stranger's. The boundary wall bent once more, at a right angle, showing me the other side of the hill and at the same time the entrance to the property. The entrance was in fact reduced to two pillars crowned with small stone lions eroded by the wind leaving their faces looking like the soft muzzles of sheep. A driveway of rowans, full of berries and birds, led to the "château", its dilapidations shrouded by a cloak of ivy. If you have lived in the Franche-Comté… yes, you have lived there. You therefore know those small but thick-walled manor houses, built to support heavy falls of snow in winter. But this one was really in a poor state. From a distance, it was impressive—an illusion—lording it over a valley, which at noon, still had its haze of blue air because the stream, sometimes underground, sometimes deep in the bed it had dug for itself, provided the conditions for such misty vapours.

Louisette stopped abruptly just before the first pillar, so abruptly that I collided with her charming back, her russet-blonde neck, her whole rounded, firm, peach-like person.

'This is as far as you can go,' she said. 'You see the spring?'

I could only partly see it, by which I mean that I could make out at the end of the line of rowans a leaping, flashing something coming from a stone niche, as if the niche, draped with shade-and-water-loving plants, were the haunt of large silver fish. I could also make out a liquid sheet of water brimming over the coping stone and doubtless running away to a pool below… but I couldn't see how I was going to slake my thirst without running the gamut of the two sheep-faced lions… Louisette went in without me, and returned carrying a small watering can, filled, with a long spout.

'You drink before me, Louisette.'

And I was not ashamed to add: 'That way I'll know your thoughts…'

But her reply was a very brisk refusal: 'I'm not *thuursty*.' It is an incomparable drink, water, when it comes, mysteriously cold, straight from the ground.

'Go back the same way,' Louisette ordered me. 'This is the real entrance, but you might be seen from the house if you went down by the main road.'

I obeyed without a word. At the spot where the wall overlooked the path by three or four metres, I felt a scatter of gravel on my head. Louisette, perched above, was watching me leave. I waved a hand, I blew her a kiss but she neither smiled nor feigned confusion. A golden head, motionlessly keeping watch amongst tufts of scabious and yellow sedum, a grave, almost unsociable stare was all I had from her that day. I remember that as I made my way down to the pharmacist's estate, I said to myself: 'She could have thrown me a flower instead of a pebble, all the same!' And I reproached that little girl, in my heart of hearts, for lacking poetry.

I will not bore you, my dear friend, by going into the details of every meeting in that, our first, week. In any case, we had no meetings, Louisette and I, properly speaking… I would climb the little mountain at around the same scorching hour of day, eleven, half past. The dryness, not the season itself, was bringing the leaves down. In my host's house, the hunters brought back bad news, of thin, water-starved game. But I barely listened. My own, very punctual game I would find wherever it might be, cool and not at all stressed by the heat, nor diminished. The strange thing was, this early stage of my adventure, which was turning out to be merely pleasant rather than exciting, was making little progress. Louisette, who laughed easily, showed no evidence of having an innate sense of fun. To be fifteen and a half, to live in extreme and dangerous solitude, probably in semi-poverty, these factors, it is true, are not the conditions for a very gay existence… to my questions she replied with only what was strictly necessary. Thus, I asked her: 'Do you live very much alone?'

'Oh, yes!' she replied.

'Doesn't that strike you as a little sad?'

'Oh, no!' she replied. 'We have visitors on Sundays. People we know.'

She added: 'Not every Sunday. That would be too much.'

Her small hands, scored with creases at the base of the fingers, told me more than she did about the heavy household chores they were set to. If they had been idle hands they would have been very pretty, and like Louisette herself, rather short, plump, the fingers turning up at the end. When she walked beside me she would break off a pointed twig and use it to clean her nails. I said to her also: 'Do you read a lot?'

She nodded, "Yes, yes," with a very capable air.

'Papa left us a large library.'

'Do you like novels? Would you like me to give you some books?'

'No, thank you.'

Her refusal was always very definite. I could not get her to accept books, or flasks of perfume, or buckskin belts, or cheap bracelets, or fine handkerchiefs… nothing, you understand? As she put it herself: "Nothing, and that's flat." This rigour was not to be relaxed for anything. "And what would *maman* say?" She fired this unvarying argument back at me in tones both severe and victorious.

'It's a terrible mother you have,' I ventured one day.

Louisette sent me the same angry look as when she had spoken of selling the stream.

'Not true. She's not a person who'd harm anyone, she isn't. If she knew I talked to you, it wouldn't go down well. All right, I'm hiding the fact I talk to you, but I have to hide it very carefully. But I put myself out to be careful, I think it's the least I can do.'

And the way she said it...! *Mademoiselle* was giving me her personal moral code, and I was the one taking lessons. To mollify and please her, I listened with an air of great respect. She stared down at me from the wall, as if she was expecting something from me, and I didn't know what she wanted or didn't want. Those of us who love young girls, we almost never risk a move unless we're sure. The one thing that disconcerts us and holds us back is simplicity, first because we find it hard to believe, and then because our success is a matter of judging the right moment. A blazing sun presided over our meetings, during which Louisette always had her eye, her ear alert for her mother, and I would return from them shattered and exhausted by the light and heat. Back at ***, I found charm and repose in playing bridge out on the flowered terrace, in a soothing orangeade, in the illustrated papers, their pages ruffled by the six o'clock breeze. Until the day I had the idea, a whole week having passed, of telling Louisette: 'I've only got ten days left here.' The corners of her mouth quivered, but she only said: 'Ah!'

'Alas, yes! And the squire of *** is organising a series of motor excursions, picnics in the region's beauty spots... I won't always be able to go off by myself. But if, instead of roasting up here, I came to enjoy the coolness on this little mountain in the evenings, might I not meet you then?'

I assure you I made myself exceptionally timid, a wonder to behold, and I didn't even try to hold her hand. My reward was surprising: she looked alarmed, bit a nail, fiddled with her hair, removing and replanting those dreadful metal pins in her chignon, from which the finer hairs escaped like smoke from a fire. She darted a look all round, blurted out: 'I don't know, I don't know…' and her raised arms wafted to me the incense of a woman's scent. I made it look as if I was hesitating, then as if I lost my head, and I seized the cushiony Louisette by her slender waist. I spoke into her hair, under her ear: 'This evening…? Six o'clock…?' and I refrained from kissing her on the lips before striding swiftly away. I plunged down amongst the trees before she could have time to call me back, or even think of it, and I was already far away when I realised we had not uttered a word that conveyed tenderness, desire or friendship.

Dear friend, I pause, but not simply to empty this glass of water. No, thank you, I am not tired. When one talks about oneself one is never tired until one has finished. But I can see about you an air of apprehension, not to say disapproval. Why? Because my heroine's age is no more than three months short of sixteen? Because I have allowed my eyes to fall on too young a flower? Don't be too quick to judge me, and certainly not to lavish your pity on the tender lamb. It is my turn to find you hard to understand. At fifteen, and even less, a princess used to be paired off with an heir to some throne, without causing anyone any offence. At thirteen, queens used to get married. To seek justification in higher places than royal thrones, do I need to remind you what, at fifteen, Juliet understood by "listen to the nightingale"?* If my memories are accurate, was it not at sixteen that you yourself declared you were in love with a bald man who, at forty, looked twice as old? The description is yours, I believe. Tender shoots have their place, so our fathers used to say, with easy-going tolerance. I claim the same indulgence, yours anyway, as a man who was, apart from an occasional exception, a passionate admirer of tender shoots almost all my life, without ever having blackened their good name or impregnated any of them. So, I shall resume my account, which you provoked, and I shall lower neither my eyes nor my voice.

I had requested a meeting then, at dusk; but because of my deliberately speedy departure, I was not certain that Louisette would be there to meet me. I did meet her, however, in a landscape made new by the hour of the day, amongst long shadows that stood out from each other and made the low mountains seem higher. You know the area, you know that as the daylight wanes the valleys fill with a very different colour from the blue of midday. The periwinkle blue, the lilac slashed with bright yellow and dark green, the hilly, complicated terrain that the fierce light of noon had thus far concealed from me, the smell of wood fires being lighted for the evening's soup, I found it all enchanting, and I was not in the least bored as I waited for Louisette. To be frank, I was already sufficiently consoled for not seeing her, when she arrived, running, and threw herself, as if in play, into my arms, where she was very happily received. I immediately admired the way she had, by this precipitate arrival, avoided all those old chestnuts: "It's you at last", or "Ah, how wonderful!" Whatever social level she belongs to, the female creature leaves us with a very narrow choice of welcomes. So Louisette threw herself breathlessly into my arms, as if she was playing "tag" and had made it to safety. She laughed, unable to speak, or at least she seemed to be unable to speak. Her wretched iron hairpins fell from her pretentious little chignon, and around her head hung her natural hair, not very long, but fanning out and catching the fiery light thanks to its thick curls. And as for her heaving chest, I assured myself, with a cupped hand, that it was genuine. Our physical intimacy became established in no time at all, to a degree beyond my hopes, in ways quite new to me. I say physical, for want of being able to say intimacy, pure and simple. I believe that an ordinary man, I mean an ordinary lover, would have thought he had met in Louisette the most shameless of semi-peasants. But I was not an ordinary lover.

I gave Louisette time to calm down before offering her kisses, which she received naturally, eagerly… do not raise your eyebrows like that, dear friend: do I surprise you as much as all that? Yes, eagerly, in a way a male lover might have acted, careless and hurried, as almost all of them are. But I was not a careless lover. Louisette surrendered then to the pleasure of being kissed, and in the pauses, she smiled, looked me full in the face, with joy, as if she was thrilled to have found the real way of conversing with me, of no longer being in difficulties with a stranger. Dusk had fallen, but high in the sky was a long streak of cirrus still catching the light of the sun, and there on my arm, which was supporting Louisette, I could see a happy face, exuberant hair, eyes not modestly half closed but wide open, the whole picture reflecting the colour in the cloud. It was very beautiful and I missed no detail of it, I can assure you. Someone called, from the direction of the house, and Louisette sprang away from me, depriving me of her firm little mouth, her narrow, rounded waist, her feet that I was nursing in my hands. She listened, waited for a second shout, strained ears and eyes to locate the exact point where the summons had come from, and disappeared at top speed, with no more farewell than a hurried wave of the hand.

That evening I made mistake after mistake at the bridge table. Once away from Louisette, I could more readily admit I was rather disconcerted. In her presence—you may rightly suppose I saw her again the very next day—I allowed myself to be guided by my experience but also by Louisette herself. Without revelling in many details which would embarrass us both, I confess I had never encountered anything resembling Louisette, as much for her simplicity as for the mystery she represented. To be clear what I mean, I think the sensuality of a grown woman, if she were to behave as Louisette did, would have been hateful to me. Louisette was greedy in the same way that children are criminal, with grace, with majesty. Physical confidence is always beautiful to see. Louisette's sheltered her from the ultimate dangers, it is true, but it needs to be said that she was lucky in chancing on me and not someone else. She enjoyed her pleasure as a legitimate gift, but nothing led me to believe that she had any experience of it, before me. This strange adventure outlasted the fine weather and detained me, not at all conveniently, at the house of my friend the luxury-loving former pharmacist.

After two weeks, I was telling myself: "That's enough. Any more would be too much." Perhaps, deep down, I was… what shall I say? I was shocked, I was… well, a little put out that the little pony brought in from the field did not reward me with any show of… for heaven's sake, just a little sentiment, a little…

I beg your pardon, dear friend? Excuse me, I am not a brute—as I proved, at least once every twenty-four hours—and I didn't think it was asking too much to hope that a softer, contented Louisette would finally treat her disinterested lover as a friend. So much so that one day I was the one—under the effects of a very understandable agitation—I was the one who said to Louisette, leaning closely over the little shell of her ear: 'You won't completely forget your old friend when he is far away?' I was sitting on a large block of granite made softer by a covering of lichen. Louisette, sitting lower down, was leaning her golden head against my side. She lifted her rosy face, looked up with eyes which, at that moment, were as clear as could be beneath their brown flecks, and I thought I was about to hear for the first time… a kind word, a guileless remark, a sigh… she simply said: 'Oh, no!' She sounded exactly like children asked by an imbecile parent the imbecile question: "You don't love daddy more than you love mummy, do you?", and I left her that day sooner than usual, though she gave not the slightest sign that she noticed the fact. We talked so little… she listened to me, certainly. But she listened far more attentively to noises I couldn't hear, and would signal me, sometimes sharply, to be quiet. Especially one day… I was in the middle of telling her heaven knows what, to give myself the illusion that we were having an enjoyable conversation together; and seeing the steady gaze of her fine speckled eyes, her half open mouth, whose fresh pinkness I had just reinvigorated, I felt flattered by her attentiveness. She was lying propped on one elbow, and we were nestled in one of those miniature clearings to be found up among the heather on the high ground. I was seated, leaning over her, and she began to flutter her eyelids, succumbing to a lassitude that filled me with pride. One of the charms of Louisette was to confess, out of nowhere: "I'm hungry" or "I'm sleepy", to yawn when she needed food, to fall asleep all of a sudden, deeply asleep, for a moment or two. So, she was fluttering her eyelids, her reddish lashes flickering with fire at every blink, when without warning she opened her eyes wide, sat up, seized me by the shoulders and catching me by surprise forced me down against the ground, where she pinned me with unexpected strength. I tried to struggle upright, but she threatened me with a raised fist and her childish face looked fearsome. The whole thing lasted only the space of a dozen heartbeats… then Louisette let go of me, her cheeks and lips turned white and she fell limply back on the dry grass. Regaining colour, she explained: 'Your head was sticking up. There was someone on the track.'

'Who?' I asked.

'Someone from round here.'

I think she had recognised her mother's footstep. She adjusted without embarrassment her open blouse. Everything she let me see of herself would have rejoiced what they call a "*bon vivant*". In contrast to the *bon vivant* and the libertine, it was for me a serious matter to see how far the state of childhood and a pure, knowing womanliness can overlap. By way of adornment to so many beauties, nothing more than simple cotton underclothes, a small blue ribbon, plain stockings… no other perfume than the slightly russet fragrance of the hair. In moments of emotion, I could detect on her the scent of that plant… what is it…? that spiny plant with pink flowers… it smells of perspiring blondes… restharrow, thank you. When I was away from Louisette, I used to think about what she might have been, which is always a stupid exercise. I dreamt of remodelling her, of discovering her, I imagined her as the nymph crouched over her stream, and naked as she deserved to be… we do not elevate ourselves to great heights when we fancy ourselves bringing art and literature into the religious sentiments inspired in us by a beautiful body.

After a few days, Louisette changed the times of our meetings, and for the benefit of my host I had to play the poet and nocturnal rambler in order to be able to walk up to the "château" at about ten in the evening. 'Why so late?' I asked my little friend.

'Because *maman* goes to bed at nine. She gets up before five, all year round. In the evenings at eight thirty I've just finished clearing dinner away and everything. After that, I can do as I like, provided I'm very careful.'

'You don't sleep anywhere near your mother then?'

She lowered her reddish-blonde eyebrows: 'Quite near… I can show you…'

She led me to the entrance with the lions, along the narrow path which she followed as if it was broad daylight: 'The square tower, beyond the spring… there's only one room on each floor. *Maman* has the top one and has given me the other because it's the better one. But as soon as it turns cold, *maman* brings her bed down into my room, which is warmer. The cold comes early, in this part of the country.'

She fell silent. I could hear the stream and its imaginary fish leaping in their pool.

'But, Louisette, dear, isn't it dangerous for you to go out at night…?'

'Yes,' she said.

So distant was that considered, almost gloomy "yes" from the cry of a woman in love who rushes headlong into danger, that I stifled my gratitude. A "yes" that manifestly showed no thoughts for me. She was looking vaguely towards the squared gable, and the leaping silver of the spring, at the end of the drive. It was an evening of misty moonlight, pink and vaporous. This close to the "grand entrance" we could have been seen. But I fully trusted my little companion, who fortunately knew how to keep us invisible, making me walk close against the boundary wall, drawing me into the opaque shadows of a laurel, which left its scent on one's hands. We only encountered passing creatures of whom she was sure—a soundless dog, guiltily out hunting for its own benefit; the grey horse belonging to the "château", which limply trailed its chain, taking advantage of the mild night… the misty moon projected few shadows, but from time to time it emerged from its halo, and I could see before us my long shadow, welded to a shorter one.

Don't you get the feeling I'm telling you a rather sad story…? It's odd, so do I. Yet the story of Louisette starts off as being something rather charming, don't you think? But this evening I seem easily cast into a wistful mood. In any event, it's in the nature of adventures of this kind that they quickly grow old, lose their freshness. Or alternatively, to keep them going and retain a little spice, they need to put us, the devotees of a certain type of women, in the clutches of young demons; and indeed they do exist, yes, in no small numbers. Louisette was merely a girl coming into bloom, a young girl for whom I represented an agreeable distraction, for I was not so foolish as to believe I was teaching her anything about the facts of life. With country girls, there is rarely such a thing as physical innocence. Louisette accepted, indeed she determined, the character of our relations. She almost never accorded me my first name; when she did call me "Albin", it felt borrowed.

I always had the feeling that she was trying hard not to call me "*Monsieur*", and I wouldn't have been put out if she had. Quite the opposite. This reserve only increased the sense of wonderment—and I would add, the appetite—that Louisette inspired in me.

One day, I brought her a little ring, a bauble made of shiny glass, a child's plaything, and catching her by surprise I slid it on her finger. She went as red as… a nectarine, as a dahlia, as whatever's the prettiest and deepest red in the world. But it was from anger, would you believe. She wrenched the ring from her finger, thrust it brutally back at me: 'I have already commanded you' (she said *commanded*!) 'not to give me anything!' When I had taken back my modest jewel, contrite, she checked that the little cardboard box, the tissue paper, the blue ribbon had not been left on the lichen-covered rock where we were sitting. Bizarre, don't you think?

But on the other hand, I could only take pleasure in such a vivid little idyll, and one so in keeping with my natural inclination. If Louisette's reluctance to speak was merely down to a lazy mind, I had met other slow-witted creatures, and less pleasant ones than her. All the same, I could feel at moments, flowing from her to me, something resembling sadness. I felt sorry for a destiny as uncertain as Louisette's. And then my holidays, a scorching experience twice over, were having the effect of leaving me rather weary. I was growing impatient at being unable to fathom a damsel prepared to roam the woods, at night, with me, but who jumped as if someone had shouted: 'Fire!' and went pale and trembled all over if she heard the footsteps or voice of her mother…

All that, my dear, belongs to the past, but a past that has

remained buried. I cast new light on it as I tell you the tale, since it seems to me, yes, it really does seem my adventure is not as cheerful a one as I thought. At the time, I sometimes wondered if Louisette wasn't taking advantage of me the way a libertine takes advantage of a complicit girl. That idea irritated me to the point where I had a brief and unexpected burst of pure rage. Not in front of her, but at bridge, with my host, one evening when I had not arranged to meet Louisette. Nobody noticed anything, except that I played very poorly. I was listening to the sound of the wind, which for the first time since my arrival, seeped in under the doors and brought to us from the open terrace—it was very mild—the poignant smell of imminent rain, of flowers after the flowering season is over. The song of the wind, the scents of autumn, I knew they both presaged my return to Paris, and the fact disturbed me to a degree I found quite unexpected. I thought about my departure, about the existence, in winter, of two women in the draughty "château", I made myself imagine the rowans without their leaves, green on one side, silver on the other, without their clusters of red berries, the spring sealed over by frosty weather, its living water trapped under great discs of translucent ice…

I went to bed early, and rest, greatly needed, resolved everything. The next day I awarded myself a long, idle morning, spent in a rocking chair on the terrace, in banal conversation. I felt released from that worried and indiscreet emotion which drew me towards the hidden life of Louisette. Indiscreet, I use the word advisedly. Did she not herself consider it so, since I was still, after four weeks of daily meetings, waiting for any show of feeling on her part? I found it agreeable simply to listen, to look at my surroundings, to treat, *in petto*,* the guests who gathered round the table, all of them about fifty, like myself, as old men, because they were married and potbellied. The day slipped by rapidly, mild, purged of the recent great heat, and so calmly that I scarcely gave Louisette a thought. But you know all about the dangers of an amorous habit; it is of the same order as tobacco addiction, or dependence on drugs. When the hand on the inevitable Louis XIV clock face hoisted its elaborately wrought point towards a tortoiseshell figure X, I could hold out no longer, and I rose to my feet.

'What, again, Chaveriat?' my host said. 'Even tomcats don't go out when their bellies are full.'

'I am not a tomcat,' I replied, 'I am a martyr to self-care and vanity. If I don't take at least an hour's exercise after meals, I would lose my waist and my flat stomach.'

'Take care, the weather is about to change.'

'When it's a full moon? Highly unlikely. After my defeat last night, find another victim.'

Nevertheless, I took a rainproof coat and my pocket torch, which Louisette would not allow me to switch on when I came anywhere close to her "château". A Gustave Doré moon* seemed to leap from cloud to cloud, to plunge behind patches of cumulus ringed with fire, emerging from them naked, brilliant, a little round-shouldered. These rapid switches of light and dark in the heavens told me the wind had risen, and I promised myself I would stay no more than a few minutes with Louisette. It was a wise decision. Just as I reached, at the spot where the boundary wall stood at its highest over the footpath and afforded it the deepest, most shadowy protection—the spot where my little friend used to wait for me—just at the moment when I was closing my arms around a very dear body, as beautiful standing up as lying down, never gazed on freely enough, never used freely enough, just at the moment when the mutual kiss of greeting confirmed, in the darkness, a presence unrivalled in its physical realities, its elastic qualities abandoned to my loyal care, the wind rose in a dry rush. I held my companion all the more tightly. Just from the feel of her invisible hair and her raspberry lips, of her already open blouse whence rose to my nostrils the assurance that it was a woman I was holding to me and not a child—I could have divined her colouring of pink and russet. The vague remorse of my day-long indifference towards her accentuated my fervour. God knows where remorse of this kind might lead us…! Have no fear, dear friend, that last phrase heralds no digression. I use it to indicate that I was very close indeed, that evening, to behaving like a normal thorough-going brute, like a man who has only one way of approaching the woman he desires. And I am not sure that Louisette, as overexcited as I was, would have stopped me.

It was at that instant that the rain, sweeping across the land, descending through the scents of the undergrowth and the insects that believed summer had returned, dropped on us. Rain in sheets, rain like a collapsed ceiling, diluvian, overwhelming. I flung my waterproof coat over Louisette, and very deftly she draped half of it over my shoulders, but what covering could ever have been adequate? The downpour ran in waterfalls beyond the hem of the coat and drowned our feet. Louisette hesitated no longer, she dragged me away. The diffused light from the masked moon showed me we were passing the lions guarding an absent set of gates, the rowans, the spring lashed by a vertical torrent; I felt paving stones under my feet, and I leaned over Louisette's streaming ear to make myself heard above the drumming of the rain: 'I'll see you tomorrow, darling… go back quickly!'

But she kept hold of my hand and led me on, I felt dry flagstones under my feet, a different atmosphere, less noisy, enfolded me and I understood, from the denser darkness, that I had crossed a threshold, the threshold of the "château" of Louisette.

Through the open door the light from the stormy night came in only weakly. Driven further inside by the vertical curtain of rain, I breathed in the air of those country house hallways, where one hangs up old straw hats, where one leaves one's rubber boots and stacks the first fallen fruit…

'I can't light a lamp or a candle,' Louisette whispered. 'Give me your hand.'

Leaving the door wide open, she led me to one of those long wickerwork settles, uniformly uncomfortable, that you find as often in Provence as in the manor houses of Brittany. A long, thin padded cushion covers their seat without making it any better. You had one when you lived in Brittany, around 1908. We sat down. Feeling with my hands, I checked the downpour had not drenched the thin clothes Louisette was wearing. And if she shivered, it wasn't from cold. But my determination to seize the initiative was constrained by the unfamiliar surroundings and the total darkness; I was as wary of one as of the other.

'As soon as the rain eases off, you must go,' Louisette whispered.

To myself I added that I would need no second bidding.

And I arranged Louisette against me, in a perfectly unobjectionable manner, her feet stretched out on the empty part of the settle, her head against my shoulder. She slipped her arm beneath mine, and we remained there, not moving. Gradually I was able to make out the dimensions and arrangement of the vestibule: a wooden-balustraded staircase rose from the floor just behind us; a bunch of pale flowers grew clearer on a largeish table which I could touch if I reached out a hand; a window with no blinds slowly took shape as a blue rectangle to my right. I strained eyes and ears, and I clenched my jaws. No doubt everything that was worrying to me was reassuring to Louisette, whom I could feel relaxed and warm against my arm and as motionless as a little hare crouched in a furrow.

'I think the rain is easing off,' I whispered in her ear.

Hardly had I spoken when the deluge doubled in force and the darkness thickened around us. I can't tell you, dear friend, how badly I wanted to flee that place. I was about to make my mind up and I was already anticipating, as if it were a pleasure, being forced to make a dash, behind the beam of my pocket torch, for a house where I would be safe, when I noticed, from the slackness of her little body, that Louisette had dozed off. I have told you how, with the promptness of healthy constitutions, she gave way to the beckoning of hunger, sleep and other feelings… I nearly woke her up, but it was such a novel situation to have her leaning on me, asleep, that I wanted to wait just a little longer. I was, if you follow me, I believed I was in the position of her protector, for the first time… and I too shut my eyes, to give the brief illusion of resting lovingly side by side. But at the slightest creak or crack I opened my eyes, and God knows, just about everything creaked and cracked in that wreck of a house!

A vague glimmer of light fell on us, and I wanted to wake Louisette to tell her both that the moon had come out again and that I was leaving. But I noticed the light was not coming from the open doorway, nor from the window on my right. It was far worse: the light began to move and lit up some sort of landing at the top of the staircase. There is a noticeable difference between electric lights and others. This was a lamp flame, I could not doubt it, coming towards us, and the shadows of the banister poles began to turn slowly within the cage of the stairs. I called, quietly, into the bush of damp hair covering my shoulder: 'Louisette! Someone's coming!' The girl gave a terrible start, and I sat up to... Oh, yes, definitely, to flee, but she clung to me with the strength that had once forced me down in the heather. All I succeeded in doing was to make a crashing noise of feet, settle and table, and the only thing that sprang to my lips, my goodness, was the first syllable of a hearty curse. The shadows of the balusters completed their rotation on the walls, and there appeared, lamp in hand, a woman, rather small, in a mauve dressing gown tightly tied in the middle. Her resemblance to Louisette left me in no doubt, and with no hope. The same wavy hair, though already almost completely white, faded features, which would one day be Louisette's, and the same eyes, but with a searching and magnificent look in them which Louisette would perhaps never have, a look that did not tremble with anguish, which was determined to see everything, to know everything... how prolonged such a moment can be, and how does the boredom, yes, the pure boredom, a yawning boredom, of having it all come to this, how does such profound boredom force its way into the mere split seconds of such a dramatic moment? And the little idiot, who was still clinging to me, who would not let me go… with a twist of the arm, I tore my sleeve from her fingers and I stood up. I remember that I said: '*Madame*, don't be frightened…'

And then I came to a halt. The girl, still stretched out on the settle, had propped herself up on one arm like *The Wounded Gladiator*.* And with her bent elbow she swept her hair back. She did, poor girl, what she had to do, she called for help: '*Maman!*'

And she began to cry. The surprising thing is that I was hardly moved by it at all, because, in spite of my exasperation with everything and with myself, I was put on the spot by the appearance on stage of the principal character in this scene, the mother. She put down her paraffin lamp, turned to Louisette and said: 'So, this is the man, is it, daughter?'

The girl lifted her head, showed her wet eyes, her mouth forming a square like young children when they are crying, and called: 'No, *maman*, no, *maman!*'

'Don't make so much noise, my girl,' said the woman with white hair. 'Nevertheless, this is indeed the man who has been leading you astray these last few weeks. You I've seen, yes. I saw you with him in the little coppice near the heath. But as for him, I'm not displeased to set eyes on his face, no, I'm not displeased…'

She swung round rapidly to face me. The lamp standing between us was unshaded, but she did not blink. I couldn't help noticing the contrast between the expression on her face and her last words. I thought I ought to break my silence… my biggest concern, and you can't imagine how large it loomed at this unexpected juncture, was deciding what was the most acceptable thing to do or not do in such cases… the decision I made was not the best…

'*Madame*,' I said, 'in spite of appearances, which look very bad, I can give you my word that I have not behaved, towards… towards Mlle Louise, in such a way as to…'

The lady with white hair placed her two fists on her hips. This fishwife's posture did her no disservice, on the contrary.

'In such a way as to…' she echoed.

'In such a way as to put her in a position…'

'What a mouthful,' she interrupted drily. 'I'm well aware what it means. You think it is an excuse. Not me. Am I supposed to say thank you?'

The girl's sobbing stopped. At the same time the downpour tailed away, and this double hiatus filled the room with a great stillness which seemed to be waiting for my response. It is very rare that a man awaiting judgement is not tempted to lose patience and commit some foolishness… that is what happened to me.

'Uh! *Madame*, I am not a saint, I admit, but I forced no one against their will here, and the beauty of your daughter…'

The feet of the cane settle, pushed backwards, scraped the flagstones and Louisette stood before me, her eyes aflame through her unwiped tears.

'I forbid you to speak to my mother in that tone,' she said in a low, rough voice.

'Oh!' I said. 'If I've got both of you against me, I prefer to…'

And I made as if to withdraw, an action never completed because the haughty little lady was standing between the door and me and she did nothing to unblock my exit.

'You are not here to inform us of your preferences,' she said.

She really had the most admirable eyes, her cheekbones and the bridge of her nose were burnished by the sun and the wind, and she was glaring at me fit to pierce my brain, so much so that I riposted: 'In that case, *madame*, if you would be so kind as to tell me in what terms I may offer you an expression of my regret…'

'*Monsieur*,' she interrupted insolently, 'may one know your age?'

If I was expecting a question, it was certainly not that one. Besides, I was astonished that this strange mother, finding her daughter with a man, did not resort to any of the classic arguments and abuse. She had a mouth made for vehement words, a fluency of expression somewhere between the peasant and the bourgeois. Her preposterous question caused me, in confusion, to perform a whole series of idiotic gestures, such as running a hand through my hair, hitching up the leather belt at my waist and ostentatiously drawing myself up to my full height to show myself to good advantage: 'I do not see, madame, what my age has to do with any of this. Nevertheless, I will consent to inform you that I am forty-nine.'

For a moment, I thought she was going to laugh. Why not turn this scene into a humorous joust? The good woman seemed endowed with a certain wit, and was far from timid. A kind of laugh did indeed flit across her features. She caught her daughter by the arm, pulled her close, mixing her white hair to the other's red, and whispered passionately: 'You hear him, daughter? You see him, that man there? Daughter, daughter, he's three times as old as your fifteen and a half, and even a bit more! You've been led astray by a man of fifty, Louise! A young lad from around here, and there's plenty, I could understand that. But a man of fifty, Louise, a man of fifty! Ah, you should be ashamed!'

If I hadn't held myself in check, I'm telling you, I would have swatted these two country bumpkins aside, and how! They were staring at me, their two heads together, their two countenances similar. And that blinding, unshaded lamp… the older one released the arm of the younger, held out a hand, pointing a brown and wrinkled index finger at me, and raised her voice: 'If your father was still alive, my Louise, he would be exactly the same age as that man there!'

Louise gave a sharp little cry and hid her face in her mother's fleecy white locks. The mother did not push her away but continued to speak: 'Yes, you don't want to see him anymore now, and high time too, Louise! But you need to look at him! Look at him, the man born the same year as your father!'

With her hand buried in her daughter's hair, she turned her face in my direction. As if she had been brandishing a decapitated head, she gripped her by the hair so hard that the girl's eyes were stretched up slantwise.

'The man who would have been fifty years older than his child, if he had made you pregnant, Louise!'

At this ringing remark, Louisette pulled away from her mother and did indeed look at me. The all too vociferous lady had not finished with me, and she no longer respected the silence of the night: 'You see what he has on the sides of his head? White hair, Louise, white hair, like mine! And those lines under his eyes! Everything about him says he should be out to grass, my girl, out to grass!'

She shot this rustic expression at me with an air of murderous glee, a delight that made me crumple. Louisette stood there, stupid and serious, like children who have just woken up, the flames of the lamp reflected yellow in her eyes. She refastened her opened top, pulled the folds of her jacket straight, adjusted the buckle of her belt, and spoke quietly to her mother: 'Do you want me to chase him off, mother? We can "*chaase*" him off, the two of us, do you want to?'

Before the mother had time to answer I hurled myself out of the door. Yes, out of the door, and the devil himself couldn't have kept me in. You don't understand? You don't understand that I would sooner do anything than join battle with a woman—or two of them… fist fights between men, even war, frighten us men, make us less nervously afraid than a woman's fury. We have no idea what might happen when a woman is in a rage. We never know if she is going to treat us as a "miserable cur", with a display of lofty dignity, or try to rip our nails out, remove our noses in one savage bite. Nor does she, what's more, she has no idea. It all surges up from somewhere deep down inside her. Oh, I ran like the wind. And I was very careful, careful of the loose stones, careful to avoid the ruts. If I could eventually laugh at my misadventure, I certainly couldn't then. The platform leading up to the house, the spring, the drive lined with rowans, the pillars with lions, I rushed past them in a dream. I outpaced my two pursuers and took the narrow path round the outside of the boundary wall. But the moon had travelled across the sky and now its light illuminated the path. At a clump of scented laurels, I stopped. I could no longer hear the sound of running feet behind me and I forced myself to breathe slowly while contemplating, to prove to myself how unflustered I was, the valley, which had turned pale blue again, curling with tepid mists, pierced with silver birches whose satiny trunks gleamed as if it were daylight. I mopped my forehead and neck, and reaching for a cigarette I found my hands were trembling.

A sudden sense of danger sharpened my unease; I looked up and just above me, just behind the top of the crumbling wall, I saw the mother and the daughter, from the waist up, watching me. Only with the greatest of effort did I not take to my heels and flee. I reprimanded myself, and adopted instead the leisurely gait of a nonchalant stroller dreaming beneath the moon. A pair of heads, side by side, followed my movement: they were still after me. Indeed, the two heads appeared further along, and waited for me. White hair and blonde hair floated in the air like the seeds of poplars.

Seeing them quite still above me, I stopped. I have done less difficult things in my life… then I began to walk again, slowly, on the descending slope of the path. I passed beneath the two women… it was then that a fair-sized lump of stone fell from the top of the wall, brushed my shoulder, rolled at my feet and tumbled down the track ahead of me. I stepped over it and continued on my way. A little further on, a second stone just like the first grazed my ear as it fell, before giving me quite a bad bruise on my toe—I was only wearing canvas shoes. I came to a spot where the wall had partly collapsed, reducing its height. My tormentors were standing on the breach and waiting for me. A righteous anger, the anger of a man offended, finally overwhelmed me, and launched me into an assault on the breach and the two silly geese defending it. In three bounds I was up there. Doubtless they too recovered their good sense and an appreciation of their condition as females, for after a moment's hesitation, they fled and melted into the abandoned garden, behind the feathery outlines of fruit trees and the tufty fronds of a clump of asparagus ferns.

No matter! I had recovered my self-respect. I stood there. I shouted God knows what threats in the direction of the fleeing pair. I grabbed a stake which I brandished like a sword. It was ludicrous, but it made me feel much better. Afterwards, I scrambled down to the path again and reached the track under the trees, splashed with moonlight like a leopard's skin. Rabbits hopped out of the way and I scared off a number of birds. But I was trembling far more than all these small creatures. My nerves did not betray me altogether, however; I dabbed at my bleeding ear and began to hobble because of my bruised foot.

The following day, I succumbed to what they call a "healthy" dose of fever, attributable, I think, to the damp, mild air, to the unwise decision to go out without a jumper… to emotion as well, I am not so stupid as to deny it. No encounter has ever taken me aback as thoroughly as the one with that moralist, the little lady with the frizzy white hair. That an indignant mother might claim, for example, some sort of compensation, fine, that is logical—that she might even require the supreme reparation, marriage, fine again. A demand of that sort always ends in some gentler solution. But this particular mother, with her fleecy head, her eyes, her way of charging the enemy… she would have stoned me to death if she could. Yes, yes, she would have done it. Without risk to herself because who could have accused her of anything? A wall that was already collapsing of its own accord… the girl, I think she was a bold and adorable idiot.

And so my bout of fever was long and punishing, with episodes of shaking that made the bed squeak, dreams, even a touch of delirium—my nerves have always been highly-strung. I saw cats, yellow and ferocious, twin heads supported on a single neck. My host looked after me with impeccable thoughtfulness. He fortuitously found in one of his drawers some "homemade" analgesics. He made a hole in one of my slippers so that the bruised toe and its swelling had enough room. And a kindly female relative sewed on to my pyjamas several religious badges of proven repute.

No, I did not see Louisette again. I did not try to see her. I had suddenly lost all taste for evening strolls in the Franche-Comté, for the gleaming bark of silver birches, for little clearings up on the heathland. But there was never any question of forgetting her, and with good reason. Whenever I thought about her, the cold, the heat, the bouts of nausea, the distortions of my dreams returned in a rush and extinguished her charms. And far worse, my dear: the most beautiful… no, the most hideous fear of my life reared its importunate head to insinuate between skin and blouse, between Louisette and me, between other Louisettes and me, its icy little serpent, its drop of scalding wax, and ever after to rule out for your old friend—look, I'm damp with perspiration just thinking about it—every Louisette on this earth… what's that you say? A punishment for my sins? Wait! An unexpected sort of compensation did come my way. You know the outline, exploited scores of times in literature and anecdote: the enemies and victims of

Don Juan arrange a switch, so that in the curtained bed where some beautiful prey should be waiting, there lies in wait instead a duenna or some overripe chambermaid. And the next day the chorus of jokers gathers round the seducer and with great delight informs him… informs him? Did he not know anything, then? Had the evidence of his own senses not told him? Do they suppose that without those mocking fingers he would have risen the following morning, very content, from the warm darkness of the bed? It is quite possible. You may assume, then, my dear, that in place of the Louisettes I have still been able to avail myself of the chambermaid. And since I had no friends to go and shout it from the roof tops, I have never complained overmuch of my fate.

THE GREEN SEALING WAX

At the age of fifteen I was in the grip of a mania for "stationery supplies". I was only imitating my father, for whom the mania lasted all his life. At an age when every vice clings to the adolescent like burrs with their hundred hooks caught in one's hair, a girl of fifteen risks running into more than one form of danger. My seemingly enchanted freedom left me exposed to everything, and I believed that freedom to be total, unaware that the maternal instinct, in Sido, disdained such methods as spying and proceeded through moments of sudden illumination, leaping telepathically to wherever peril lurked.

When I reached fifteen, Sido gave me the most startling proof of her second sight. She divined that an unimpeachable man had designs on my sharp little face, on my long tresses, which fell to my knees, on my well-formed body. Having entrusted me to the family of this man over the holidays, she received a warning as vivid, as overpowering as the sudden gift of faith, and she cursed herself for having delivered me into the hands of strangers. Immediately, she donned her little bonnet with its drawstrings, climbed aboard the rickety train—they were putting ancient coaches on to a brand new line—and found me playing in the garden with two other little girls, under the gaze of the silent man, leaning on his elbows like the meditative Demon at Notre-Dame.

Such a spectacle of domestic peace could not deceive Sido. In addition, she noticed that I was prettier than I was at home. Girls, whether fifteen or thirty, take on fresh colour in the warmth of masculine desire. I had done nothing that could merit any reprimand, and Sido took me away, and the irreproachable man never dared to ask the reason for her arrival, nor for our departure. In the train, I saw her fall asleep, weary like a victorious warrior. I remember that lunch time came and went and I complained of being hungry. Instead of blushing pink, looking at her watch, promising me my favourite treats of brown bread, cream cheese and red onions, all she did was shrug her shoulders. My famished craving was of little importance—she had saved the most precious thing.

There was nothing guilty, or complicit, in my relations with this man, unless through inattention. But the perils of inattention are much more serious than overexcitement, wild laughter, blushing, the clumsy coquetries of fifteen-year-olds. Only a few men create this effect of torpor, from which girls awake to find themselves lost. The surgical intervention, so to speak, of Sido restored all things, myself included, to order, and I had one of those relapses into childish ways which the adolescent, ashamed and intoxicated at the same time, succumbs to with relish.

My father, born to write, left few pages. When the moment came to begin, he frittered away his energy fussing over his writing materials, arranging round him everything the writer needs and a vast array of the superfluous besides. Because of him, I am not immune to the same compulsion. As a result of having admired, coveted, the inventory for the perfect work table, I still insist that certain bureaucratic requirements be met. Adolescence being a time when nothing is done moderately, I stole from my father's table a small mahogany set-square smelling of cigar boxes, then a ruler in white metal… as well as receiving a reprimand, I felt the full force of a little grey eye blazing into mine, the eye of a rival, after which I did not attempt a third theft. I confined myself to prowling, full of evil thoughts, round the treasures of his stationery store. A blotter to lean on, unused, an ebony ruler, one, two, four, six crayons, sharpened with a penknife and in various colours; nibs for writing round hand, nibs for writing in italics, nibs for writing figures, drawing pens no bigger than a blackbird's feather; sealing waxes, red, green, purple, a hand blotter, a bottle of liquid glue, without prejudice to the transparent amber-coloured patches known as "lick and stick";—the tiny remnant of an old army coat, reduced to a scrap, frayed at the edges and used for wiping pens—a large inkwell, flanked by a small inkwell, the pair of them in bronze, and a shallow shellac bowl filled with a golden powder for drying ink; another bowl contained small lumps of sealing wax in many colours (I ate the white ones); to the right and left of the table, reams of paper, some of it laid paper, some with lines, some watermarked and of course that little gadget which bit into the paper, and when you pressed its jaws together, embossed the white sheet with the name: *J-J Colette*. There was also a beaker of water to wash brushes in, a box of watercolours, an address book, bottles of ink, violet, red and black, the mahogany set-square, a pouch to hold compasses, the tobacco jar, a pipe, the spirit-lamp for sealing letters…

A landowner seeks to expand; my father in turn tried to plant out on his vast table propitious new crops. At various times one found on it a mechanism which could cut through a wad of paper a hundred sheets thick, and frames primed with a white jelly which drank in the wet ink, in mirror image, and then reproduced copies of the original, blurred, faint and watery. But my father rapidly tired of them and the big table was restored to serenity, methods once more classical, and disturbed by no inspiration. On it were strewn its fruits, covered in crossings-out, its cigarette stubs and its preliminary drafts, screwed into a ball. I am forgetting, God forgive me, to mention the paper-knife department, three of four made of boxwood, one in fake silver, the last in yellowing ivory, with a crack running from handle to point.

From the age of ten I had consistently coveted these material goods, conceived for the glory and convenience of the human brain, which fall under the general term "stationery supplies". Childhood only takes real pleasure in things it can keep hidden. For a long time I found my seat of pleasure in a corner at the left-hand end of the big bookcase, which had two sections, upper and lower, and four doors (it was sold under a court order). The doors of the upper section were glazed, those of the lower, plain wood, handsome, figured mahogany. By opening the lower door at right angles, it could be made to meet the side of a chest of drawers, and since the bookcase left a small length of unclaimed wall, I would shut myself in, sitting on a small foot-stool, in a four-sided cubbyhole formed by the side of the chest of drawers, the wall, the left-hand end of the bookcase and its opened door. In front of me, on three mahogany shelves, were spread some laid paper with a dish of golden powder and the icons of my religion. 'You can see where she gets it from,' Sido would say, laughing at my father. It is touching that, with every tool to hand, my father only rarely settled down to writing anything, whilst Sido, finding any old surface, pushing aside an invading cat, a basket of plums, a pile of washing, or else setting on her knees in the guise of a desk a copy of Littré's dictionary, Sido wrote. A hundred marvellous letters bear witness. To continue, or finish, a letter, she would tear a page from the kitchen accounts book, and cover the back of a bill…

And so she had little reverence for our useless altars. But she did not discourage me from treasuring, from beautifying my office, for amusement. She even proved to be concerned for me when I revealed to her that my cubby-hole was becoming too small for me… 'Too small… yes, much too small,' she said with a wan look. 'Fifteen already… where is Darling-Minet going to go, too big for her hideout, like a hermit crab driven from its borrowed shell by its own growth? I've already plucked her away from that man of impure thoughts. I've already had to forbid her from going dancing on the dance floor on Quasimodo day.* Already she's escaping and I shan't be able to follow her… already she wants a long dress, and if I let her have one, the blindest of people will realise she is a young woman; and if I refuse, everyone will stare at her woman's legs under her too-short skirt. Fifteen. How can I stop her turning sixteen, then seventeen…?'

Sometimes, in those days, she would come and lean over the mahogany flap that isolated me from the world. 'What are you doing?' She could see very well what I was doing, but she didn't understand it. I refused to give her the answer all those other creatures she observed generously gave, the bee, the caterpillar, the hydrangea, the mesembryanthemum. But at least she could see that I was there, in a safe place. She indulged my obsession. Those sheets of beautiful glossy wrapping paper, I had them for covering books, and from her pieces of gold braiding I made bookmarks. I had the first pen-holder furnished with a mottled glaze, turquoise in colour, that appeared at Reumont's the stationer's.

One day my mother brought me a small stick of sealing wax and I recognised the stub of green wax, pride and joy of my father's office… no doubt I considered the present disproportionate, since I did not shout for joy. I squeezed the wax in my hand, where, as it warmed up, it gave off a faintly oriental smell of incense.

'This,' Sido said, 'is a very old wax, and you can see it's speckled with gold. Your father already had it when we were married; he inherited it from his mother, and his mother claimed it was used by Napoleon I. But one has to bear in mind that my mother-in-law lied every time she opened her mouth, so…'

'Is he giving it to me, or have you taken it from him?'

Sido twitched. She became irritable when she thought she was being forced to lie, and when she tried to avoid an untruth.

'When are you ever going to stop twisting a curl of hair

round the end of your nose?' she exclaimed. 'It's a perfect way of getting a red nose, a big fat one like a bigaroon cherry! That wax? Let's assume your father is lending it to you, that's all. Now, if you don't want it…'

My ferocious possessive grab at it made Sido laugh again, and she said, affecting light heartedness: 'If he needed it, he'd ask for it back, obviously!'

But he did not ask me for it back. The green wax, flecked with gold, scented my narrow, mahogany-walled empire for a few months and my pleasure became less sharp, as do all pleasures that are not disputed. Besides, my sense of vocation for all things writerly was on the wane, for a while, under competition from a fashion crisis. My new desire was to wear the "curvaceous look", that is to say, to reshape my flat behind into an apple by adding a cushion of horsehair, which as a result lifted the hem of my skirt up at the back. The brutality of adolescence made the girls of thirteen to fifteen in my village into fanatics who stole horsehair, cotton and wool, rolled rags up in a bag and attached the terrible fixture known as "false behinds" over one's hips, on a dark staircase, out of sight of their mothers. I also wanted a curly fringe over my forehead, leather belts tight enough to cut off my breathing, boned collars, essence of violets on my handkerchiefs…

After that, I relapsed once more into childhood, for a female creature takes several goes, stopping and starting, before she blossoms into full flower. I relished being an ugly duckling, long hair gathered in a twist and the rest drooping flatly on my cheeks. Rather than any adornments, I preferred my old lace-up shoes, the aprons I wore for school, their pockets full of hazelnuts, pieces of string and chocolate. Bramble-lined paths, clumps of bulrushes, liquorice shoelaces, cats, in short everything I still love today, became very dear to me again. There are no words to hymn, no exact memories to illustrate periods like this, which from a distance I can only compare to deep ravines of happy sleep. The smell of haymaking sometimes brings them back, perhaps because, yielding to the fatigues of growing, I used to fall dreamlessly asleep, for an hour, in the new-mown hay.

*

At this point there occurs the episode which for a long time was called "the Hervouët will affair". Old M. Hervouët died, and no will was found. The district was rich in fantastic characters. Under the old tiled roofs, yellowing with lichen, in the freezing drawing rooms, the dining rooms left in eternal darkness, on the parquet floors sown with traps in the form of knitted rugs, along the paths of the kitchen gardens, between the hard heads of cabbages and the frizzy parsley, any small town, any village had a proud roll-call of things that cannot be explained. My village accepted without great surprise, indeed with a degree of deference, the behaviour of the Gatreau boy, an admirable exemplar of the romantic madman, who was able to rave away in perfect safety, a wooden cigar between his lips, who had a twitch that sent his head and its black curls jerking in all directions, and who fixed on young women the long stare of his narrow Arabian eyes. Then there was a woman who had chosen to lock herself away in her house, and who waved hello through the window, and passers-by admired her: 'That Mme Sibile hasn't set foot outside her bedroom for twenty-two years! My mother saw her, exactly where you see her today. And you know, there's absolutely nothing wrong with her, it's a fine life!'

But Sido, a brisk walker, hurried me on still quicker when we passed the aquarium wherein swam the lady who had not been out for twenty-two years. Behind the clear glass of her window, the prisoner smiled, a linen bonnet on her head. Sometimes her small yellow hand would be holding a cup. A sure instinct for what is horrible and forbidden kept Sido away from that ground floor window, from that floating head. But the sadism of childhood put to her, through my mouth, a score of questions: 'How old do you think she is, Mme Sibile? Does she sleep at night beside the window in her armchair? Does anyone undress her? Does anyone wash her? And how does she go to the toilet?'

Sido started as if stung by a wasp: 'Be quiet! I forbid you to think of such things.'

M. Hervouët had never counted as one of those eccentrics to whom a town extends its mildly sniggering protection. For sixty years he had been, with his landowner's handsome income and his terrible clothes, a distinctly eligible prospect, and then a decidedly well-off married man. After being widowed, he had remarried, to a former postmistress, thin as a rake and full of fire.

When she struck herself on the breastbone, saying: 'It's a raging furnace in here!' her dark Hispanic eye seemed to hold you responsible for some incurable fire within. 'I'm not a timid man,' my father used to say, 'but I'd rather face the hounds of hell than be left alone with Mlle Mathiex!'

Once remarried, M. Hervouët no longer went out. With

the result that no one knew precisely when he developed the stomach complaint that was to carry him off. He was a man clothed in all weathers in black, including his cap with flaps. A hairy man, his head a fleece of white cotton wool, his beard the same, he looked like an apple tree that had fallen prey to the woolly aphid pest. High walls and the almost permanently closed double doors of the coach entrance formed a protective screen round his second joy. A single climbing rose tree dressed three sides of his double storey house in blossoms every summer, and the thick garland of wisteria on the top of the wall fed the early bees. But no one had ever heard it said that M. Hervouët liked flowers, and if we occasionally caught sight of him coming and going, black beneath the hanging clusters of wisteria and the showers of rose petals, he seemed neither responsible for, nor connected with such a flourishing of blooms.

In the translation of Mlle Mathiex to Mme Hervouët, the former postmistress lost none of her yellow and black wasp-like traits. A matt skin, a pinched waist, a handsome, inscrutable eye, tight on her nape a mass of severely tamed hair, dark, touched with white, she showed no surprise at becoming a well-to-do bourgeoise. She seemed to like growing flowers. The fair-minded Sido considered it only right to take an interest in her, lent her books, accepted in exchange cuttings and young arborescent violets of a blue that was almost black, whose stems rose bare from the earth like a minuscule palm tree. I had no sympathy for the person or manner of Mme Hervouët-Mathiex. I was vaguely scandalised by the way, while serving up remarks of irreproachable banality, she expressed them in exaggerated tones of supplication and plaintiveness…

'What do you expect,' my mother would say, 'she's an old maid.'

'But *maman*, she's married!'

'Do you think,' Sido retorted crisply, 'that you stop being an old maid for a trivial reason like that?'

One day, my father, returning from his daily "stroll round town", which, as an amputee, he did to preserve his vigour, said to my mother: 'Here's some news! The Hervouët relatives are attacking the widow.'

'No?'

'And with red-hot bullets too! They say the grounds for their accusations are extremely serious.'

'A new Lafarge scandal?'

'You're very greedy for scandal,' said my father.

I thrust my sharp-pointed face between my parents: 'What's the Lafarge scandal?'

'A matrimonial horror,' my mother said. 'Every age has them. A famous case of poisoning.'

'Ah!' I cried, full of enthusiasm, 'how exciting!'

Sido looked me up and down with a stare that disowned me.

'And there you are,' she murmured. 'That's what they're like, at this age… daughters should never be fifteen…'

'Sido, are you listening or not?' my father interrupted. 'The relatives, manoeuvred by a Hervouët niece, claim that Hervouët did not die intestate, and that his widow has caused the will to disappear.'

'If that's the case,' Sido observed, 'you could accuse every widow and every widower of anyone who dies intestate.'

'No,' my father came back, 'people who have children

don't need to make a will. The Hervouët lady's charms enflamed Hervouët only from the waist up, seeing as…'

'Colette,' my mother said to him sharply, indicating me with a glance.

'So,' my father resumed, 'she's in a fine pickle. The Hervouët niece says she saw the will, saw it with her own eyes, she even described it. A large envelope, with five seals of green sealing wax flecked with gold…'

'Fancy that,' I said naively.

'…and on the title page the words: "To be opened after my death in the presence of *Maître* Hourblin or his successor."'

'What if the niece is lying?' I ventured.

'And what if Hervouët had a change of mind and destroyed his will?' suggested Sido. 'He was perfectly free to do so, I imagine?'

'The pair of you are all for the bull and against the toreador,' my father exclaimed.

'Exactly,' my mother said. 'Toreadors are generally men with bulging thighs and that's enough to make them unsympathetic as far as I'm concerned!'

'Getting back to the issue,' my father said, 'the Hervouët niece has a particularly sinister gentleman for a husband, a fellow called Pellepuits…'

I soon tired of listening. On the promise of words like: "The relatives are attacking the widow!" I was hoping for bloodthirsty ambushes, and all I was hearing were snatches of mumbo-jumbo such as "discretionary quotient, holograph will, deposition of complaint against X…"

At best, my curiosity flickered back to life when the widowed Mme Hervouët paid us a visit. Her short, imitation

Chantilly cape, over shoulders sloping like a Rhine wine bottle, her black mittens which allowed her fingernails to peep out, notably thick, almost opaque, the luxuriance of the black and white hair, a large reticule in black taffeta hanging from her belt and bumping against her mourning skirt; her "houri's eyes", as she called them, so many features that finally took on their particular flavour and which I seemed to see for the first time.

Sido received the widow with friendliness. Out in the garden, she offered her a finger of Frontignan wine, a triangle of Madeira cake. The June afternoon hummed with insect life, the walnut tree dropped its reddened caterpillars around us, not a cloud crossed the sky. My mother's pretty voice, the plangent voice of Mme Hervouët exchanged peaceful remarks. The only subjects, as usual, were gladioli, salpiglossis and rascally servants. Then the visitor rose to leave and my mother showed her out: 'If you will permit,' Mme Hervouët said, 'I will come back in a few days to borrow a few books; I am so alone…'

'Would you like to have them now?' Sido offered.

'No, no, there's no hurry. In any case, I've made a mental note of the titles of a few adventure stories. Goodbye, dear *madame*…'

So saying, Mme Hervouët, instead of taking the path that led to the house, set off along the one that bordered the lawn and made two circuits round the island of grass.

'My God, what am I doing… forgive me…'

She allowed herself a decorous laugh and found the corridor to the hall, where she groped, to the left and too high, feeling both door panels, for a latch she had found on the right a score of times before. My mother opened the door for her, and stood politely at the top of the steps. We watched Mme Hervouët walk away, staying close to the walls of the houses at first, then crossing the road at a trot, skirts raised, as if fording a river. My mother closed the door again and saw that I had followed her.

'She's lost,' she said.

'Who? Mme Hervouët? Why do you say that? Lost in what sense?'

Sido shrugged her shoulders.

'I don't know. It's just my impression. Keep it to yourself.'

I obeyed my vow of silence to the letter, which was all the easier to do because, imitating a larva in my succession of personal metamorphoses, I then entered the skin of an "enlightened bibliophile", and I forgot Mme Hervouët in the undertaking of a complete reordering of the bazaar that was my books and papers. A few days later, I was putting Jules Verne between *The Talking Flowers* and a relief atlas when Mme Hervouët appeared, with no bell having sounded to warn me. For we used to leave the street door open nearly all day so that the dog, Domino, could come and go.

'What a fine thing it is for a grown-up young girl,' the visitor exclaimed, 'to put the bookshelves in order. What books are you lending me today?'

When Mme Hervouët raised her voice, I clenched my teeth and screwed up my eyes.

'Jules Verne…' she read plaintively. 'You can't read his things twice. Once you know the secret, that's the end of it.'

'There's Balzac, there, on the bigger shelves,' I indicated.

'That's very hard going,' said Mme Hervouët.

Balzac hard going? Balzac, my cradle, my forest, my

voyage…? Astonished, I looked up at the tall woman in black, who stood a head taller than me. She was toying with a cut rose and staring into the air. Her face expressed nothing that might be associated with having literary opinions. She sensed me watching her, and pretended to take an interest in my writing paraphernalia: 'How charming this is. What a pretty collection!'

Her mouth had aged since the week before. She stood there, leaning over my workplace, picking up and putting down various of my treasures. She straightened up with a start.

'But I don't see *Madame* your mother?'

More than happy to move, to get away from the "lost" lady, I dashed out of the room, calling '*Maman!*' as if I had been calling, 'Fire!'

'She took away a few volumes,' Sido told me when we were alone. 'But I'd swear she never even looked at the titles.'

*

The rest of the "Hervouët affair" is associated, in my memory, with some sort of commotion, of fantastic confusion. The clearest parts of it come to me from Sido, thanks to the extraordinarily "living" sense I have even now of the sound of her voice. Her tales, her conversations with my father, her intolerant way of arguing points, of refuting them, these are the things that made me connect with a suffocating provincial adventure.

One day, shortly after Mme Hervouët's last visit, the whole municipality cried: "The will has been found!" and described the large envelope with the five seals which the widow had just deposited at *Maître* Hourblin's office. Both alarmed and triumphant, the Pellepuits-Hervouëts, other Hervouët-Guillamats, and the widow, went by appointment to the lawyer's office where Mme Hervouët faced, all alone, what Sido called "the inheritors' greedy snouts". 'It appears,' my mother related, 'that she smelled of brandy…' At this point, taking up the story instead of my mother's voice is the voice of Julia Vincent, a hunch-backed woman who came to do the ironing once a week. Over numerous successive Fridays I pressed Julia to come out with all she knew. With its nasal twang, pinched between throat, hump and hollow, misshapen chest, the penetrating sound of that voice gave me great pleasure: 'The one who was least cocksure was the lawyer. To start with, he isn't a big man, not half as tall as that woman. And she, all dressed in black, she was, and her veil covering her up all the way down to her feet. So then the lawyer takes the envelope in his hands, big as that' (she unfolded one of my father's vast handkerchiefs) 'and he passed it, like that, to the nephews and nieces, so they could recognise the seals…'

'But you weren't there, Julia?'

'No, it was M. Hourblin's little errand boy, peeping through the keyhole. One of the nephews said a few words. Then Mme Hervouët gave him a stare like a duchess. The lawyer coughed, ha-ham, ha-ham, he broke the seals and he read it out.'

In my memory, it is sometimes Sido speaking, sometimes some gossip-monger fascinated by the Hervouët affair. Sometimes, also, I seem to have an image, as if Bertall* or Tony Johnnot* had done an engraving for me, of the tall, thin woman, who never took her Hispanic eyes off the group of relatives, and who licked from her lips the taste of old *marc* brandy, swigged to give her courage…

So, *Maître* Hourblin read the will. But from the very first lines the stamped document trembled in his hands, and he broke off to clean his glasses, apologising. He began to read again and continued to the end. Although the testator declared himself to be "sound in mind and body", the will was nothing but a tissue of far-fetched ideas, among others the recognition of a debt of two million francs contracted towards Louise-Léonie-Alberte Mathiex, beloved spouse of Clovis-Edmé Hervouët…

The reading concluded in total silence and not a voice was raised from the stunned party of relatives who considered themselves the rightful inheritors.

'It appears,' Sido recounted, 'that after the reading you could hear the wasps buzzing on the trellis outside the window. All the Pellepuits and other Guillamats could do was stare at Mme Hervouët, without moving a muscle. Probably they too sensed she was lost. How is it that greed and avarice deprive people of second sight? It was one of the female Guillamats, less stupid than the others, who described how Mme Hervouët, before anyone had spoken, began to make strange movements with her neck, like a hen who has swallowed a hairy caterpillar…'

What followed after the reading spread like wildfire, in the streets, round people's kitchen stoves, in the little cafés, at the fairgrounds… *Maître* Hourblin, to the background buzzing of the wasps, had opened his mouth to speak: 'In my soul and conscience, I find myself obliged to declare that the writing in this will is not all in the same hand.'

A great howl cut him off. It was no longer widow Hervouët before him, before the relatives, but a sad fury, who whirled this way and that, stamping her feet, a sort of black-clad dervish, tearing at her face and clothing, gabbling and shouting. To her confessions of forgery, the distracted woman added several others, so packed with the names of poisonous plants like buckthorn, henbane, that the lawyer, in consternation, called out naïvely: 'Whoa! My poor lady, you're giving us far more information than anyone is asking for!'

A mental asylum swallowed up the frenzied creature, and if the Hervouët story lived on in the memory of a few people, at least there was not, in the criminal courts, a "Hervouët scandal".

'Why, *maman?*' I asked.

'Mad persons are not put on trial. Or they would need judges selected from other mad people. It wouldn't be such a bad idea, come to think of it…'

She paused, the better to reflect, from the task currently occupying her hands, graceful hands which she did not look after. Perhaps she was shelling white beans that day. Or else, with her little finger in the air, painting my father's crutches with black varnish…

'Yes, judges who would understand to what degree calculation plays a part in mad behaviour, who could tease out the kernel of concealed, fraudulent lucidity…'

The moraliser pouring such unexpected conclusions into a fifteen-year-old's ear was enveloped in a blue gardening apron, too big for her, which made her almost spherical. Her grey stare, frighteningly direct, shone sometimes through her spectacles, sometimes over the top. But despite the apron, the rolled-up sleeves and the beans, she never came across as humble, nor vulgar.

'What I do blame her for, Mme Hervouët,' Sido continued, 'is her megalomania. Dreams of grandeur are at the root of lots of crimes. Nothing exasperates me as much as imbeciles who think themselves capable of dreaming up a crime, carrying it out and not being punished for it. Doesn't Mme Hervouët's stupidity make her case all the more loathsome? Poisoning poor old Hervouët with bitter tisanes, all right, that wasn't difficult. For every guileless killer there's a stupid victim. But trying to imitate someone's handwriting, which would take a talent she hasn't got; and confidently putting her trust in a sealing wax that is rare and special, what inadequate tricks, great God, what conceit!'

'But why did she confess?'

'Ah,' said Sido, reflectively, 'the fact is, a confession is virtually inevitable. A confession is like… like what?… like a stranger you carry round inside you…'

'Like a baby?'

'No, not a baby… a baby, you know exactly the date you're going to release it into the world. Whereas a confession, quite suddenly, at the moment you least expect it, out it comes, it exults in its liberty, it flaunts itself… it shouts, it skips about… she accompanied her confession with a dance, the poor criminal, who thought herself so cunning…'

It shouts, it skips about… and so I at once released, into Sido's ear, my own secret: on the very day of Mme Hervouët's last visit I had noticed the disappearance of the little stick of sealing wax, green, with flecks of gold.

ARMANDE

'That girl? Why, she adores you, come on! She's been doing nothing else for the last ten years, what's more... the whole time you were away after being mobilised, she used to dream up pretexts to call in at the post office and ask if I'd had a letter.'

'Yes?'

'She'd never leave until she'd had a chance to ask her question: "How's your brother?" She waited. While she waited, she bought aspirin, cough mixture, tubes of lanoline, *eau de toilette*, tincture of iodine...'

'And of course you made sure she had to wait?'

'Well, why ever not? When I told her in the end that I'd heard from you, she'd go away. But not before. You know how she is.'

'Yes... no, in fact. I don't know how she is.'

'What do you want, you poor old thing? You make everything difficult for yourself, you waste your energies being needlessly delicate… Armande is an accomplished girl, that's understood. She's made a bit of a meal of her status as a rather well-heeled orphan. I grant you it wasn't an easy role to play, in a district like this. But that's no reason for you to allow her to dominate you as much as she does, you of all people, Maxime, you…! Watch out, they've made a new pavement here. At least one can get around with dry feet now.'

The September sky, dark, moonless, shone with stars noticeably shimmering in the damp air. The invisible river lapped against the single arch of the bridge. Maxime stopped, leant his elbows on the parapet.

'The parapet is new too,' he said.

'Yes. It was the shopkeepers of the town, along with the municipal council… you know, they've done very well, here, the food and clothing stores, what with all the troops passing through, and the general exodus…'

'Food, clothing, footwear, pharmacies and the rest. I also know they say "the exodus" as if they were saying "the agricultural fair" or "the gymkhana"'.

'Well, in the end they were determined to make a big sacrifice…'

Mme Debove heard Maxime give a low laugh at the word sacrifice, and she wisely curtailed her sentence to return to Armande Fauconnier.

'In any case, she didn't really abandon you, during the war, hasn't she been writing to you?'

'Postcards.'

'She sent you parcels, and a very charming pullover.'

'I couldn't care less about her parcels and her woollens,' Maxime Degouthe said violently, 'or her post cards! I never asked for charity, I don't think?'

'My God, what a difficult character… don't spoil your last evening here, Maxime! Admit it, it was very pleasant tonight, Armande is a good hostess. All the Fauconniers have always been good hosts. Armande knows how to keep in the background. There was no opportunity to move the conversation on to the children's clinic that Armande is funding at her own expense.'

'Who hasn't been more or less responsible for setting up a children's clinic during the war?' Maxime grumbled.

'Why… a lot of people, I can assure you! To begin with, you need to have the means. Well, she really does have the means.'

Maxime made no reply. He hated his sister talking about Armande's "means".

'The river's low,' he said after a moment.

'You've got good eyes!'

'It's not a question of eyes, it's a question of smell. When the water level sinks, it always smells musky here… it's the silt in the riverbed, I expect…'

He suddenly remembered having said the same thing, at this same spot, last year, to Armande. Out of disgust, she had wrinkled her nose, twisted her mouth into an ugly grimace. "As if she knew what silt was… silt, that pearly grey clay, so soft to bare toes, mysteriously scented, she thinks it's the same thing as sludge or slurry. She never misses the chance to reject anything physical, anything you can savour, touch, breathe…"

Swarms of moths were almost veiling the globes shining

at each end of the bridge. Maxime heard his sister yawn.

'Come on then, let's go. What are we doing here?'

'I could ask you the same thing,' Mme Debove sighed. 'Do you hear that? Eleven o'clock! Hector will surely have gone to bed without waiting up for me.'

'Let him sleep. We're in no hurry.'

'Yes, we are, my fine fellow. I for one am sleepy!'

He tucked his sister's arm beneath his own, as when they were students and had illusions, times when a brother and sister believe, in good faith, they are happy to act the chaste imitation of a couple. "A big red-headed chap strolls by, and the eager little sister goes after him, for the pleasure and the advantage of marrying the Grand Central Pharmacy. She was quite right, as it turns out…"

A passer-by stepped off the pavement for them and greeted Jeanne.

'Good night, Merle. Have those aches and pains gone now?'

'More or less, *Madame* Debove. Goodnight, *Madame* Debove.'

'She's a customer, Jeanne explained.

'My God, I'd never have suspected it,' her brother said ironically. 'When you put on your pharmacist's voice…'

'Tell me, do I ever make jokes about you and all your medical flannelling? "Above all, *madame*, as far as is possible, master your nerves. The improvement is noticeable, I'd even say distinct, but let us agree, yes?, to abjure the eating of meat", and I preach at you and I indoctrinate you and I drown you in sauce…'

Maxime laughed good-naturedly, so faithful was his

sister's imitation of his mildly pontifical manner. "All women are minxes, nosing their way into our vanities, our love affairs, our illnesses. The other one, Armande, can't be all that different from this one here..."

He saw her, that other one, as he had recently left her, standing at the top of the steps of the Fauconnier house. The chandelier in the hall behind her, with its blue glass and chrome hoops, transformed her into a glorious burst of morning glory. 'Goodbye, Armande...' She had merely waved in reply. "You could say she was sparing with her words all right! Just let me get her between four walls one of these days, or catch her in the woods, then I'll make her speak up, and with good reason!" But he had never met Armande in any wood. As for his capacity for violent action, he despaired of it the minute he was in Armande's presence.

Eleven o'clock sounded from the hospital, then eleven o'clock from a small, squat church, squashed between new buildings, finally eleven o'clock, high-pitched and crystalline, from the open window of an unseen ground-floor room. As they crossed the Place d'Armes, Maxime sat down on one of the benches.

'Just a minute, Jeanne! Give me a moment to settle my nerves. It's nice here.'

Jeanne Debove consented ungraciously.

'All you needed to do with Armande was set them aside, those nerves of yours. A bit of boldness is what you need, a bit of cheek. But you haven't got the nerve!'

He did not protest and she burst into malicious laughter. He wondered why the confession of sexual timidity, which provokes desire in dissolute women, gives rise to scorn in honest ones.

'She unsettles you, then. Yes, she unsettles you. I can't get over it!'

But get over it she did, to the extent of heaping on his head all manner of mockeries, accompanied now by horse-laughs, now by sniggers.

'All the same, though, you're not in the absolute first flush of youth anymore… you're not a bad man… you're not a madman… nor, thank God, are you deformed…'

She enumerated all the things her brother was not, and he was glad she omitted to mention what, simply, he was, that is, a man who had been smitten for a long time.

The long-lasting love of Maxime Degouthe, preserving him from any risk of dissolute behaviour, became a form of habit when he was apart from Armande for months at a time. A sort of conjugal fidelity allowed him, when not with her, to amuse himself as he liked, and even to forget her for periods. So that at the end of his medical studies, it was with amazement that he encountered a new Armande Fauconnier, an adult, whereas the Armande he remembered had been an adolescent all too rapidly growing taller, with pointed shoulders, at once gauche and noble like a gawky filly, full of promise.

Each time he saw her again, her hold on him grew. His feelings towards her were turbulent and secretive, like the gardener's son towards the "young lady at the château". He would have liked to sully, to bruise in some small way a girl of such beauty, whom he admired from the crown of her head to the tips of her toes, her brown hair just dark enough, her pale skin white enough, tall, lissom, like a pear. "But I wouldn't dare. No, I don't dare," he would rage on leaving her…

'The back of the bench is all wet,' said Mme Debove. 'I'm going home. Have you decided what you're doing tomorrow? You'll go and say goodbye to Armande? She's expecting you, you know.'

'She hasn't invited me to call round and do so.'

'Oh! Well, if that's your attitude! Admit it then, she's a girl who unsettles you!'

'I admit it,' Maxime said, with such unhappiness that his sister desisted from wounding him any further.

They walked in silence as far as the Grand Central Pharmacy.

'You're having lunch with us tomorrow of course. Hector would take it badly if you didn't have your last meal with him. Your parcel of phials will be ready. When are we going to get more of those serums? No one can say… so, I won't telephone Armande to say you're coming to say goodbye…? But I won't tell her you're not coming either…?'

She was spending an age fiddling in the dark with a bunch of keys. Maxime lent her the assistance of his pocket torch, whose beam caught in its circle the malicious face of Jeanne Debove, her expression of contentment and disapproval.

"She'd like me to marry Armande. She's thinking of her fortune, the beautiful, well-appointed house, the 'excellent effect' on my career, as she puts it. But she'd also like it if I married Armande without too much joy. All very normal. Except for me, since I can't bear the idea that Armande could, on her own side, marry me without love."

He hurried back to his hotel. The town was sleeping, but the hotel, close by the railway station, echoed with all the sounds inimical to sleep, shone with lights that aggravate a person's fatigue. Hob-nailed boots, swaying ceiling lights, uncarpeted floors, the gates of the lift, the groaning of water pipes under pressure, the rhythmical clatter of plates being tossed into a sink in the basement, the ceaseless trilling of a bell, relentlessly assaulted the need for silence which led Maxime to his room. Irritated beyond measure, he joined the selfish concerto of human noise, dropped his shoes on the parquet floor, carried them out into the corridor and shut his door with a violent slam.

He threw cold water over his body, dried himself off carelessly and climbed naked into bed, after staring long and hard at himself in the mirror. "Big bones, big muscles, and four working limbs, that's something already, given the state of the times. A large nose, big eyes, hair cropped short but still as thick as a motorcyclist's muffler, like the ones Mlle Fauconnier and others spend their Sundays knitting… I don't see Mlle Fauconnier sleeping with this fellow, all naked and dark…"

He could see her all too well, on the contrary. Irritated by a painful desire, he waited for the hotel to quieten down. When—apart from a stray bark, a garage door, some departing motorists—silence was finally established, a breeze got up, swept away the last offences inflicted by man on the night, and wafted in through the open window, as if in recompense.

'Tomorrow,' Maxime swore to himself. It was a muddled oath, as much to do with Armande as with the return to professional life, the daily and necessary triumph of an activity based on an essential form of indifference.

He repeated: 'Tomorrow,' flung his pillow away, rolled on to his stomach and went to sleep with his head on his folded arms, in the same attitude as a former small boy, intimidated, who dreamed of Armande with the long dark curls. So slept also, later, the adolescent who made so bold as to offer, at Peyrol's, lemon ices when "those Fauconnier ladies" were emerging from Mass. 'But no one eats lemon ices at a quarter to twelve, really, Maxime!' said Armande. In that single word "really", what a host of reprimands! 'Really, Maxime, don't *always* stand in front of the window, you're blocking the light… Maxime, really! You've played *another* ball that was out!'

But after a certain period, there were no more "*really*"s, nor reproaches from on high. Sleeping restlessly, Maxime Degouthe groped for a memory, a moment that gave his twenty-five years a little confidence and marked the end of Armande's condescension. That day, he arrived with Jeanne at the foot of the terrace steps as Armande was opening the door—decorative wrought iron—to go out. They had not seen each other for a very long time; hello, goodness, it's you—yes, my sister insisted I accompany her, perhaps it was a little indiscreet—no, really, you're joking—a friend of mine from Paris dropped me off this morning in his car—Ah! A good idea, and are you here for some time?—No, the same friend is picking me up again after lunch tomorrow.—Ah! hardly any time at all… an impoverished exchange fit to bring blushes to the cheeks of both speakers, if either of them had paid any attention to the words. On Maxime Degouthe, five or six steps below, there fell a prolonged look of surprise, of offence. He also received, brushing his knees, the swishing of a skirt hem and a bag that escaped Armande's hand and which he picked up.

After a joyless game of ping-pong, the serving of a tea consisting entirely of sugary things, an exchange of handshakes—a strong, swift, but instantly dropped hand had gripped his own—he had left Armande once again, and on the way home Jeanne had assessed the situation cynically: 'You know, the beautiful Armande could be yours without much effort. And I know what I'm talking about.' She added: 'You don't know how to go about it.' But that was the considered opinion of a woman just into her twentieth year, the infallibility of a young woman judging another young woman…

He believed he was only half asleep and was in fact dreaming deeply, but in an agitated fashion. One dreaming scene had him under the illusion, and shame, of tending to the incurable foot of old M. Queny on the steps of the Fauconnier terrace, from the top of which Armande gazed regally down. Did she not owe part of her prestige to that flight of eight wide steps, flowing up to a terrace, and which the whole town revered? "The Fauconniers' steps and terrace are so elegant… without the terrace, the house of the Fauconniers would look far less distinguished…!"

The sleeping man, as if insulted, sat up with a jerk. 'Distinguished! That cube! That great slab, with its iron-work gallery and bands of coloured ceramic tiles!' He woke up fully and the Fauconnier house once again commanded only his respect. The Fauconnier heliotropes, the Fauconnier polygonums and lobelias reasserted their identity as cultural ornaments, and to get back to sleep again, Maxime Degouthe pictured, more modestly, the duties that awaited him the next day, the day after, all his life, in the shape of old M. Queny; of Mme Cauvain senior; of M. Enfert, the father; of Mlle

Philippon, the younger, the one who was only seventy-two… for old people do not die during wars. He drank in a single gulp half his bottle of mineral water, and fell soundly asleep again, oblivious of the mosquitoes coming up from the shallow river and the sounds of the pallid early morning.

'My last day of leisure…' He breakfasted in bed, slightly shame-faced, and requested a bath, for which he had a long wait. 'My last bath… I refuse to get up before I've had my bath! I won't go before I've had my bath!' All the same, he preferred a good brisk shower, or the chance dips he had been taking in rivers and canals, from April to August…

He used, with some suspicion, an *eau de toilette* invented by his bother-in-law the red-headed pharmacist. 'Roger's perfumes, when they don't smell of squashed ants, smell of bad cognac.' He chose his bluest shirt, his spotted tie. 'I'd like to be handsome. And I'm only not bad. Ah, I'd like to be handsome!' he kept muttering as he plastered his brilliantined hair flat on his scalp. But this was a thick, rebellious crop, tending to waviness, a vigorous pelt which preferred being erect to lying down. When Maxime laughed, he wrinkled his nose, creased his yellow-brown eyes and showed his fine healthy teeth, all neatly lined up except for a gap between the front two incisors. Without his coat, and tightly contoured by his best belt, he had, as thirty approached, a pleasantly casual look, the faintly vulgar elegance which is charming in many a bicycle delivery boy, weaving deftly through a crowd like a bird in a bush. 'But with my jacket on, I look ordinary,' Maxime confirmed, smoothing the lapels of his off-the-peg jacket. 'It's partly the jacket's fault as well.' He threw a wrathful glance at his reflection. 'All the same, lovely Armande, there have been a dozen or so pleased enough with that, and some have even said thank you…' He sighed, fell back into his normal humility. 'But why remind myself of my poor little companions when the only one I want to appeal to is Armande? What does it matter if they said "thank you" and even "again"? They're not the ones I'm interested in…'

He packed his case, with the care and dexterity of a man accustomed to using his hands to work with living substances, stopping a flow of blood, applying and pinning bandages. The September morning, its flies, its warm and yellow light, flowed generously through the open window; at the end of a narrow street a dancing reflection signalled the river. 'I shan't go and say goodbye to Armande,' Maxime Degouthe decided. 'For one thing, they always lunch late at Jeanne's; then I've got my medical parcel to complete at the last minute, and if I want to have time to snatch a bite before the train, it's not possible, yes, it's materially impossible…'

At four o'clock he was opening the gate, crunching the gravel of the Fauconnier house, climbing the steps to the terrace and ringing the bell. For a second time he leant long and hard with his finger on the bell-push, a button set in a white marble rosette, but to no effect. No one came and the blood rose to Maxime's ears. 'If she's gone out, well, that's no great surprise. But where are those two so-called serving-girls and the gardener with an alcoholic's face?' He rang again, mastering a desire to give the door a hearty kick. Finally he heard footsteps in the garden and saw Armande hurrying round the corner of the house. She stopped, stood before him, said: 'Ah!' and he smiled to see her wrapped in a large, blue, bibbed apron. She untied the apron with a hasty hand and threw it on a rose bush.

'But you looked very good in it,' said Maxime.

Armande blushed, and he blushed, thinking he had perhaps hurt her feelings. "She takes it the wrong way, naturally. She's impossible, impossible! They're pretty, those specks of white soap in her dark hair… I'd never noticed, on her forehead, just at the hairline, her skin is slightly blue…"

'I was at the other end of the garden, at the wash house,' Armande said. 'It's washing day today, so… Léonie and Maria didn't even hear the bell…'

'I'll leave straightaway, I've just come for a couple of minutes… as I'm setting off tomorrow morning…'

He had followed her to the top of the steps, and Maxime was waiting for her to point to one of the cane chairs. But she said: 'From four to seven you get the full sun here,' and she led the way to the drawing room, where they sat down facing one another. Maxime took his seat on one of the armchairs decorated with stories from the fables, *The Cat, the Weasel and the Little Rabbit*, and ran his eye over the rest of the furniture. The piano, a baby grand, the clock, Revolution-period, the plants in pots, he felt reverence for them, and antipathy.

'It's nice in here, isn't it?' Armande said. 'I keep the room closed because it faces south. Was Jeanne unable to come?'

"What, is she scared of me?" he thought. He might have felt flattered, little though it was. But he looked at Armande and saw her sitting stiff and upright on *The Fox and the Stork*, one elbow on the rough arm of the chair and the other on her knee, and her hands crossed. In the half light of the shutters, her cheeks and neck took on the colour of very pale terracotta, and she directed at him her steady gaze of a well brought up young lady who knows she must not blink or look to the side, nor feign timidity in order to show what long lashes she has. “What am I doing here?” Maxime thought angrily. “This is as far as I’ve progressed, as far as we both have, after ten, fifteen years of what’s called childhood friendship. This girl is made of stone. Or she’s choked with pride… I’m not going to get trapped like this again, in the Fauconnier drawing room…” However, he responded to Armande, spoke to her about his “practice” and the “inevitable difficulties” of these years following the war. He did not fail to tell her in return: ‘But you know all these various difficulties better than anyone, burdened with responsibilities as you are, and alone in life!’

Armande broke her motionless pose with an unexpected gesture: she unlaced her fingers and dug her two hands into the arms of her chair as if afraid of sliding out of it: ‘Oh! I’m used to it… you know that my mother gave me a very special sort of education… at my age, one is no longer a child…’

Having begun in assured tones, her sentence ended on a puerile note that belied its last words. She regathered her composure, her voice changed: ‘A glass of port, dear friend? Or an orangeade?’

Maxime saw that she had only to reach out a hand towards a prepared tray and he frowned.

‘You were expecting guests? I’ll be on my way!’

He had risen to his feet; she stayed where she was and put a hand on Maxime’s arm.

‘I don’t invite anyone on a wash day. I promise you. Since you told me you were leaving tomorrow, I thought you might think of…’

She stopped, pulling a little face that Maxime did not

appreciate. "Ah, no! Don't go and spoil that mouth for me! That line of the lip that's so precise, so full, and those corners of the mouth that are so… so… what's the matter with her? You'd think she was burying the devil today!"

He realised he was looking at her with inexcusable severity, and forced himself to be cheerful: 'So you were undertaking serious household chores today? What a pretty laundry maid you make! And all the children in your clinic, have you got them under your thumb yet?'

Only his lips were laughing. He knew very well that with Armande he was made sombre by love, jealous, artificial and incapable of melting away, between himself and her, an obstacle which perhaps did not exist. Armande breathed deeply, squared her shoulders, commanded her whole face to be no more than that of a pretty brunette, regular and calm. But three shadowy creases, two at the corners of her mouth, one on her chin, etched themselves into her smile, and trembled at the least emotion.

'I have twenty-eight children at the farm, you know?' she said.

'Twenty-eight children! Don't you find that's a lot for a young woman?'

'I am not afraid of children,' Armande said gravely.

"Children. She likes children. She'd be magnificent, pregnant. Tall as she is, she'd swell up beautifully, without going all round and squat like little fat women. She'd fill a huge space in the garden, in a bed, in my arms… there would be confidence in her eyes at last, the beautiful tired eyes of pregnant women. But for that to happen to her, *mademoiselle* would have to tolerate the idea of someone coming near her, and a bit closer than to offer her a ball at arm's length on a tennis racket. She doesn't look as if the idea has ever occurred to her, no, she doesn't. In any case, it won't be me, I give up!"

He stood up, his mind decided.

'This time, Armande, it's serious.'

'What?' she said, her voice hushed.

'The fact that it's five o'clock, I've got two or three urgent things to do, a large parcel of medicines to prepare… my little village is short of everything pharmaceutical, serums, pills…'

'I know,' Armande said quickly.

'You know?'

'Oh! I overheard someone saying so, by chance, at your brother-in-law's…'

He had bent towards her a little, she shied away so fearfully that she banged her elbow against a tall and solid standard lamp.

'Have you hurt yourself?' Maxime said coldly.

'No,' she said in the same tones, 'not at all.'

She walked in front of him to open the door with its metal grille, which resisted.

'The wooden frame has warped… I'm always telling Charost to see to it…'

'Hasn't it been like that ever since I've known it? Leave my childhood memories intact!'

She was shaking the door, tight-lipped, with a stubborn force that made the glazed panels rattle. A crashing of glass and metal exploded behind her, and turning round, she saw Maxime stagger on the smashed bulb holders and the chrome-plated branches of the chandelier, which had just come away from the ceiling. Then he bent weakly at the knees and fell on his side. On the floor, he sketched a half-formed gesture with his hand and did not move again.

Armande, with her back to the door, which she had not had time to open, stared down to where, at her feet, the man lay on his bed of shattered glass. She said, haltingly: 'No…?' incredulous. The sight of a slick of blood trickling down behind Maxime's left ear and stopping for an instant at the blue collar of his shirt, which began to absorb it, gave Armande back her voice and her ability to move. She squatted down, sprang up again, opened the door half blocked by the injured body, and sent her piercing cries into the garden: 'Maria! Léonie! Maria! Maria!'

The cries reached Maxime in the unconscious state where he lay. Along with the cries, he started to hear the buzzing of beehives and sounds of someone hammering, and he half opened his eyes. But he was immediately overcome by weakness again and fell back among the hammering and the swarming bees, where pain, in its turn, arrived to find him. "The top of my head hurts. It hurts behind my ear and in my shoulder…"

Once again, loud yells disturbed him: 'Léonie! Maria!' He came to, reluctantly, opened his eyes, received full in the face a shaft of sunlight, seemingly red and interrupted by a twin, shifting shape. At once, he understood that Armande's two legs were pacing back and forth through the beam of light. He recognised the feet of Armande, the shoes of white canvas and black leather. The feet were pacing in every direction on the carpet close by his head, sometimes stopping at a strange angle and tottering, sometimes side by side, and they were trampling on the glassy debris. He felt the farcical urge to untie one of the white laces, but at the same moment he began to experience a stabbing pain, and involuntarily moaned.

'My darling, my darling…' said a voice with a tremor in it.

"Her darling? What darling?" he wondered. His cheek, which he raised, was lying on shards of pale blue glass, on broken bulb caps. The blood spread, feeling gluey on his cheek. The pathetic sight of the precious scarlet expanding in all directions woke him fully and he understood everything. Seeing the two feet turning their heels towards him and running out to the terrace, he took the opportunity to put a hand gingerly to his painful head, his bruised shoulder, and find the source of the blood behind his ear. "That's all right, a large cut. Nothing broken. I could have had my ear sliced off. Lucky I've got good thick hair. My God, I've got a headache."

'Maria! Léonie!'

The black and white feet returned, two silk-clad knees dropped to the shattered glass as if in genuflection. "She'll cut herself!" He made a vague movement, in an effort to sit up, then chose to remain still and quiet, having turned his head sideways to let Armande see the location of his wound.

'My God, he's bleeding…' said Armande's voice. 'Maria! Léonie!'

There was no response, nothing.

'Ah, the hussies…!' the same voice said viciously.

From sheer astonishment, Maxime twitched.

'Speak to me, Maxime! Maxime, can you hear me…? My darling, my darling…'

There came the sound of wooden clogs running up the garden; they clattered up the steps.

'Ah! There you are, Charost! Yes, the chandelier has come down… you could die here and no one would notice! Where are they, those other two?'

'In the meadow, mademoiselle, hanging out the sheets… Oh! The unfortunate young man! He had a hundred years of life ahead of him!'

'I'm sure he still has! Run round to Doctor Pommier, tell him… if he's not there, Doctor Tuloup. If he's not there, the pharmacist, yes, the ginger-haired fellow, Mme Jeanne's husband. Charost, go and fetch the towels from my bathroom, the hand towel from the cloakroom, you can see I can't leave him… and the brown box, in the wardrobe! And hurry! Tell those two idiots to leave their washing, don't go yourself, send someone!'

The clogs made off, resounding like clanging bells.

'My darling, my darling,' the low, soft voice said.

"That darling, it *was* me," Maxime told himself. Two warm hands questioningly felt for one of his, pressed it delicately. "But my pulse is perfectly strong, come along! Don't panic, don't panic. She must look so beautiful just now…" He groaned deliberately, snatched a rapid glimpse of Armande through his eyelids. She was ugly, with huge, terrified eyes, her mouth gaping and stupid. He squeezed his eyelids tight, much cheered.

The hands pressed a wet towel over his wound, pushed the hair aside. "That's not the way to do it, little friend, that's not the way… don't they have any iodine then in this Fauconnier place? She's going to make me bleed even more, without doing any good; but who cares about that, so long as she's concentrating on me?" The ferruginous smell of the iodine came to his nostrils, he became aware of the good sharp sting, and abandoned himself, well pleased. "Very good! But as for putting an effective bandage on, my girl, I don't think much of your chances. That will never hold. You need to shave off a bit of my hair…" He heard the young woman click her tongue against her teeth, "tt, tt", then she wailed: 'Oh! I'm too silly! Drat it all!'

He had to prevent himself from laughing and murmured something vague and plaintive.

'Maxime, Maxime!' she pleaded.

She undid his tie, unbuttoned his shirt, and feeling with her palm for his heart, brushed the male nipple, which stood up proudly. For a moment, both of them froze, each remaining as perfectly still as the other. As it withdrew, the hand to which the heart had given its reassuring response, made the same journey in reverse. "I could take this hand, caressing me now and quivering in astonishment, get up, embrace this good and beautiful girl whom I love. And if only she could be, instead, the injured person, the groaning one, then I could console her, rock her in my arms… it's what I've longed to do, for such a long time… but what if she struggles, pushes me away…?" He resolved to prolong his deception, stirred feebly, spread his arms and fell back, feigning insensibility.

'Oh!' Armande cried. 'He's badly hurt! Those imbeciles, why don't they come?'

She leapt to her feet, ran to fetch a raffia seat-pad which she tried to slip between Maxime's head and the splinters of glass, and the makeshift bandage came away. Maxime heard Armande stamp on the floor, turn in circles, slap her thighs in an access of powerful and undignified despair. She returned to him and sat down squarely among the debris of glass and blood-streaked water, propped herself, half lying, beside the injured man. With delight, he sensed she was losing control and he could hear her weeping. He squeezed his eyelids tight so as not to see her. But he could not avoid the scent of dark hair, of heated skin, of sandalwood, that aura of a healthy brunette. With a finger, she drew back one of his eyelids, and he rolled his pupil to the top of his eye, like someone in ecstasy or a faint. With her sleeve, she wiped his forehead and his mouth, furtively she parted his lips, leant over to look at the white teeth, the gap between the front two. "Any more of these little games and… and I'll gobble her up!" She leant a little lower, adjusted her mouth to Maxime's and instantly jumped back, horrified to hear the sound of running footsteps, of breathless voices. But her entire body remained next to his, tamed, watchful, and she still had time to whisper the hackneyed words of rudimentary lovers that girls stammer, while waiting for the man to teach them others or to invent more beautiful and more private ones for themselves: 'Darling… my beloved pet… my own Maxime…'

When the rescue party arrived, she was still sitting on the floor in her wet skirt and torn stockings. Maxime was able to return to consciousness, round off his lie with a few inconsequential words, smile at Armande with a distracted air, and protest at all the fuss being made around him. The Grand Central Pharmacy had provided its stretcher and its pharmacist, who wound round Maxime's head a turban of bandages. Then the stretcher and its accompanying *cortège* set off, wafted on its way by a chorus of voices: 'Open the other door… careful, it won't go through! I'm telling you, it will, if you lean to the right a bit… it fits by a millimetre… you've eight steps to go down.'

On the terrace above, Armande stood alone, no use any more and as if forgotten. But from the bottom of the steps, Maxime summoned her, with a gesture and with his eyes: "Come… I know you now. I have you. Come, we shall finish that fearful little kiss you began. Stay with me. Confess all…" She came down and gave him her hand. Then she adjusted her pace to that of the stretcher-bearers and walked submissively, all blotchy and rumpled, as if she was emerging from the very arms of love itself.

A WEDDING

Gathering over one arm the white train of my dress, I stepped, alone, into the garden. The fatigue of a long day, its early start coming after a night lost to wakeful reflection, was finally bearing down on me.

It had been a small, very modest affair, my wedding. A timber merchant from our neighbourhood, his wife and his daughter; the groom's two witnesses, Adolphe Houdard and Pierre Veber.* No Mass, a simple blessing at four in the afternoon. At five, Sido was resting for a moment, stiff in her black silk dress with its jet adornments. Her complexion was noticeably red, as happened whenever she felt unhappy and was trying to hide it. My father, in his armchair, was reading *La Revue bleue*.* Pierre Veber and Houdard, along with my youngest brother,* had gone off to play billiards in the back room of a small "drinking establishment" in the neighbourhood, dark and cool.

Was there ever a more low-key wedding? It was not without its strange features though. In the first place, all photographers, even amateur ones, had been banished. The bride failed to wear the queenly satin, the coronet of wax flowers. A muslin, sprigged with tiny flowers, gathered at the neckline, gathered at the waist, a broad white ribbon tied round the forehead—"Vigée-Lebrun fashion",* my mother said—my long tress of hair lost in the folds of my long skirt, I can see nothing more to say about myself, other than that I looked very nice, and pale.

However modest in personnel, the wedding procession was rich in beards. What a lot of facial hair, in those days, on male countenances! My brother the young doctor, like the charming Pierre Veber—twenty-six years old, brown eyes flecked with gold, and with all the grace of pampered sons—like Houdard and my husband, wore their beards pointed, sculpted with scissors, and my husband's moustache, an opulent blond roll with pointed ends, justifiably stood out as exceptional; he had acquired it at Le Mans, in the 31st Artillery Regiment.

Unsteady on my ready-made white satin shoes, I soon sat down on a step. From the house there drifted to me the voices of my husband and my elder brother. One had shrugged off his morning coat, the other his frock coat. In total disregard of this sacred day, they were busy devising witty miniature fables.

'Yours is better,' my husband was saying. 'My one, "*Mauri, tu ris, tes saluts tentent*,"* doesn't have the same general appeal. If we could come up with two more by tomorrow, before the train goes… say it again?'

I heard my brother declaim:

'Une mine est béante, un champ qui la domine
'Glisse, et soudain s'engouffre avec un long fracas.
'MORALITE:
'Garde-toi, tant que tu vivras,
*'De jucher les champs sur la mine.'**

'Brilliant! And what have you got for my "Poetry Corner"?'

'Nothing, apart from old man Hugo:*

'When the child appears, the family circle
'Applauds with cries of acclaim...

'and warmly congratulates Mme Lachapeigne, first-rate midwife, who has just brought to a successful conclusion the happy labour of childbirth…'

'I've got another,' I shouted from a distance. 'I've got a Baudelaire!'*

'Sois sage, ô ma douleur, et tiens-toi plus tranquille.
'Tu demandais le Soir, il descend, le voici...

…but it will now appear over six pages, with two daily serials signed by the public's most admired names… will that do?'

'Bravo! Bravo!' my husband said joyously. 'You are the perfect little comrade-in-arms!'

I was proud of this name, which he had been calling me since I was sixteen.

'Haven't you finished in there, you two?' I shouted.

'No,' my husband answered. 'And what's more, who's

ever heard of a village where the post goes at five and wedding breakfasts start at six thirty? I'm still looking for something for my "Literary Corner", something nice and hackneyed from Sully Prudhomme*… I adore you.'

I wrapped my train, which was annoying me, round my white stockings and waited patiently. A childhood and adolescence structured round the lives of my two older siblings had accustomed me to occupying a minor place in things, to making little fuss, and to being used to young men's amusements, amongst which I include witty word games such as irreverent pastiches, puzzles, puns and satirical acrostics.

In the village where my elder brother practised medicine, I used to cling to the company of my own family, but I had developed a tender admiration for the prestigious and very Parisian journalist, as noted here, son of a school friend of my father and fifteen years older than me. The admired friend, having become my fiancé, had been my husband for approximately an hour and a half…

I got to my feet, nibbled a leaf from the mint, sat down again on the edge of a glazed frame for germinating seeds, pulling my skirt up over my slightly damp underskirt and its decorative frill of lace. Our cat, with her tricolour markings, crawled out from under the canvas sheet where she was gradually melting in the heat, and the vigorous smell of the tomato plants, half crushed by her siesta, emerged with her.

The intoxication of a girl in love is neither as constant nor as blind as she wishes to believe. But her pride keeps her mute and brave, even in moments when she might give a great cry, timely and sincere, the great cry of realisation and fear. That cry had not risen to my lips, for two long years of being engaged had established my fate without changing anything in my life. Once he had become my fiancé, this family friend came to see us, not all that frequently, bringing books, magazines, sweets, and departed again… the great event of our engagement, for me, had been our correspondence, the letters that I received and wrote in abundance.

When he left us, I would accompany him to the station to catch the tiresome stopping train. After which I would retrace the kilometre walk with the dog Patasson. I would pretend not to hear the disobliging comments of my brothers—what brothers do not mildly curse, do not mock the fiancé who is taking a sister from them? Mine, to test my patience, talked about him without using his name, calling him just "He".

'Did you notice,' Achille would say to Léo, 'how he's grown taller since last time?'

'Taller? Are you sure?'

'What do you mean, am I sure? His cranium sticks out now, above his hair!'

'Are you two going to pipe down?' Sido said. 'Do you really mean to hurt the little one's feelings?'

'It's very good for her,' the older brother replied. 'She'll see other things like that when she's married. She'll be prepared.'

He was telling the truth. I would bite the inside of my cheek and affect disdain. In recompense of a sort, my brother announced to no one in particular: 'I have to go off on my rounds. It'll be a hell of a trip… Adon, Montcresson, Saint-Maurice…'

I never needed to make him say it twice. And when the moment for departure came and he tossed his doctor's bag on to the seat of the cabriolet, he was sure to find me installed there with my book, my cold snack, my old coat, ready for the long journey, for the hills we would need to walk up to spare the mare, resigned to hearing the loud "Hooo-là… hooo-là…" of the pregnant women, and always mindful to scoop up a handful of unripe oats or wisps of hay to keep the mare happy, in short, returning to the habits of my childhood…

Feeling limp and weary at the end of that 15th May, 1893, the bride was passing the time enlarging, with the end of a stick, the exit holes of an ants' nest. The pink sun rose up the walls of the house; the fatigue of that day left me feeling drunk; and also the discomfort of having spent every hour since early morning gazed upon by eyes that were assessing the risk I was taking. How does it turn out like this, so little anguish, so little poetry? But my poetry beforehand was composed of solitude, independence, my family trait of unsociability, and since the morning, everything had been intent on denying me these things… "Tomorrow I'll put my everyday dress on again, the one that suits me best, and I will accompany my fiancé to the station with my brother… tomorrow…"

'Couldn't you just leave us a bit of the table for our papers?' protested the voice of my brother.

I could hear the clinking of cutlery and crockery being set out in the main room, on the big table. The long dusk was falling, without relieving the unseasonal heat. I called for Sido with looks and words but she made no response. Since morning she had been avoiding me as if turning her back on a scandal… "Tomorrow, on our way back from the station, we'll go round by Les Croches, because it's prettier. We'll take the milk churn…"

The generic family term “we” was still the only pronoun I could use. Tomorrow the stopping train, which it took an hour on the horse-drawn “public omnibus” to reach, would carry me off, married, to Paris.

Between the tomato plants needing to be set upright again and the tricolour cat, did I then have the moment that convinced me both of my courage and the mistake I was making? Girls going through that moment when the scales fall from their eyes are not to be pitied. The next moment makes them face up squarely to their illusions.

Time having passed, our guests returned, multiplying the sounds of voices. ‘To-table-to-table!’ my father commanded.

‘Toot-able, toot-able!’ my second brother replied, who must have been a little tipsy. The single young maid of honour appeared at the top of the house steps, dressed in iridescent taffeta and changing colour like a pigeon, and I stood up to go in, pausing to embellish my bridal corsage with a posy of dark red carnations, in precocious flower under the glass frame and smelling of essence of cloves.

‘My god!’ exclaimed the young girl in iridescent taffeta. ‘Would you mind removing that?’

‘Why? It’s pretty, and they smell nice.’

‘Very pretty,’ Sido approved. ‘All that white is so dull. And naturally my daughter doesn’t look particularly bright today. Girls normally do have papier-mâché faces on their wedding day.’

‘It’s hard not to…’ began Mme N…

‘Easy enough,’ Sido retorted. ‘All they have to do is not marry.’

‘Do as I say and not…’ murmured the charming voice of

her son-in-law, freshly acquired if not fresh in years. For Sido had been married twice.

Many memories of that far off time are lost to me, all the fellow guests at the wedding breakfast are dead, except the bride with the corsage blooming with red carnations, and perhaps the maid of honour in iridescent taffeta. I think the menu for the meal was simple and very good. But of what came between the pike in mousseline sauce and the dessert—bastions de Savoie, towers of nougat decorated with a trembling rose in spun sugar—my memory has passed on nothing. For thanks to a few mouthfuls of champagne, I fell into the sudden slumber that overcomes exhausted children at table. It appears that my head came to rest against the back of my chair and stayed there. Mme N… was seized by a second crisis of indignation, Sido having insisted, with a vindictive emphasis directed at everyone and no one, that I should be allowed a moment's sleep. For a few minutes I slept, and I heard as I awoke my husband's voice: 'She looks a bit like the Beatrice Cenci* in the Barberini Palace*…'

'What she really looks like, with her red carnations,' said Pierre Veber, 'is a dove someone's stabbed in the breast with a dagger…'

Sido's voice became aggressive: 'Can't you think of anything better to say than compare her to a decapitated woman and a wounded bird?'

A second later, her superstitious hand, in slipping a white shawl over my shoulders, plucked the carnations from my corsage and woke me up properly, just in time for me to be requested to perform the ritual dispensing of the Savoy confection, to knock down the nougat tower, to destroy the poor green and pink rose with blows from a silver trowel…

The next morning, a thousand leagues, chasms, discoveries, metamorphoses beyond retraction separated me from the day before. In the hour before our departure, Pierre Veber enacted a pantomime *corrida* in the open street, helping himself to the precious red tartan shawl of Sido to make passes as with a cape. And on that following day, I left for Paris, in an old carriage that rattled with all the clatter of a stagecoach, in the company of three men whom I scarcely knew, but one of whom had just made me his wife. The joy of returning to Paris—and also, I think, the farewell champagne toasts—made them delirious with gaiety. Corpulent and agile, as he always was, my husband bounded from one luggage rack to the other with astonishing lightness. Houdard, from the depths of his black beard, modelled on Sadi Carnot's,* sang, and Pierre Veber patiently dismembered the mechanism of the alarm bell. Then they calmed down, and carelessly fell asleep as the night was closing in.

From time to time, I pressed my cheek to the window to make out, on the horizon, the vague glow that would announce we were approaching Paris. But all I met with was the darkened reflection of my own face, and behind me those of the three strangers who were asleep with their heads lolling. I was acutely thirsty. An image, which I was carrying away with me, filled my heart with a painful swelling. My mother had sat up all night, and was still wearing, as dawn broke, her cumbersome dress of black silk and jet. Standing in the small kitchen, before the stove with its blue ceramic tiles, Sido, letting her face relapse into an expression of terrible sadness, was pensively stirring the morning chocolate.

Notes

The Soldier's Hat

Page 19 — **Paul Masson** (1849-1896): Strasbourg-born French lawyer and magistrate, who later, as a writer and journalist, was famed for his hoaxes.

Page 20 — **Marcel Schwob** (1867-1905): French symbolist writer, an influential figure among the intellectuals of his time.

Page 22 — **Maharathis**: warriors, in Hindu mythology.

— **rupees by the lakh**: a lakh is any large number, but usually 100,000.

Page 23 — **Pigeon lamp**: Charles Pigeon (1838-1915) invented the Pigeon lamp in 1884. Usually, a brass container holding petrol spirits and fitted with a glass globe.

Page 29 — **Stéphane Mallarmé** (1842-1898): French symbolist poet, 'father' of the movement.

— **Felix Fénéon** (1861-1944): French art critic, gallery owner and writer. Promoter of Seurat, Signac and the Neo-Impressionists—a term he coined.

Page 31 — **Cléo de Mérode** (1875-1966): French dancer of the Belle-Epoque, major celebrity of her time, populariser of the chignon hairstyle.

Page 37 — **"Ceres-fashion"**: Ceres was the Roman goddess of agriculture, grain, crops. In images, often shown with head covered in fruits and vines.

— **Jules Renard**: (1864-1910): a French author and member of the Académie Goncourt, best known for the autobiographical novella *Poil de carotte*, 1894.

Page 38 — **Kohler's Gianduja**: Gianduja, a chocolate blended with hazelnut butter. Kohler, a Swiss chocolate manufacturer. Charles-Amédée Kohler opened a factory in Lausanne in 1830.

Page 39 — **Pierre Veber** (1869-1942): French playwright and contributor to humorous magazines, e.g. *Gil-Blas*.

Page 40 — **charming daughter of M. de la Palisse:** Jacques de la Palice (or Palisse) (1470-1525): a French nobleman and high-ranking military officer. An epitaph to him reads: *Ci-gît* *le Seigneur de la Palice: s'il n'était pas mort, il ferait encore envie*. (Here lies *Seigneur de la Palice*: if he were not dead, he would still provoke envy.) In the script of the period, an **f** closely resembled an **s**, leading to the misreading: *il serait encore en vie* (If he were not dead, he would still be alive). In later years, many silly or witty rhymes were invented on this model. Bernard de la Monnoye (1641-1728) composed a humorous song about La Palice's supposed adventures, one stanza of which goes:

Il mourut le vendredi,	He died on a Friday,
Le dernier jour de son âge.	The last day of his age.
S'il fût mort le samedi,	If he had died on the Saturday,
Il eût vécu d'avantage.	He would have lived longer.

These verses were rediscovered by Edmond de Goncourt in the 19th Century and became popular again. They came to be known as *Palissades*, comic statements of an obvious truth. This is what Marco means by calling Colette a 'daughter of La Palisse'.

— **Jules Crépieux-Jamin** (1859-1940): French graphologist (testified at the Zola trial in the Dreyfus Affair).

Page 50 — **Khedives**: an Egyptian cigarette. Khedive is an honorific title given to Persian rulers.

Page 54 — **'A Rops!'**: reference to the Belgian artist/illustrator Félicien Rops (1833-1898).

Page 65 — **Prunier's**: Alfred Prunier (1848-1925) opened *La Maison Prunier*, the first Prunier fish restaurant, in 1872.

Page 70 — **Ville-d'Avray**: a small town, now a suburb, on the SW edge of Paris.

THE BUDDING SHOOT

Page 73 — **Curnonsky**: Maurice Edmond Sailland (1872-1956) used the pen-name Curnonsky, or 'Cur' for short. Journalist and ghost writer for numerous papers, and later, famed for his books, articles and travel guides on gastronomy.

Page 82 — **François Boucher** (1703-1770): French painter in the rococo style.

— **Louise O'Morphy**: Marie-Louise O' Morphy (1737-1814) is thought to be the model for his erotic painting *Jeune fille allongée*, known as *Reclining Girl* or *The Blonde Odalisque*, 1752.

Page 94 — **...what, at fifteen, Juliet understood by "Listen to the nightingale"?**: the reference is to *Romeo and Juliet*, Act 3, Scene 5.

Page 104 — ***in petto***: secretly

— **A Gustave Doré moon**: Gustave Doré (1832-1883) a French printmaker, illustrator and painter. His moons were frequently set in dramatic skies.

Page 109 — **The Wounded Gladiator**: now known as *The Dying Gaul*, an ancient Roman statue of a semi-recumbent warrior.

THE GREEN SEALING WAX

Page 122 — **Quasimodo day**: the second Sunday after Easter, sometimes called Low Sunday, 'quasimodo' coming from the first words of the Introit.

Page 133 — **Bertall**: real name Charles Albert d'Arnoux (1820-1882), was a French illustrator, caricaturist, engraver and early photographer.

— **Tony Johnnot**: real name Antoine Johannot (1803-1852), was a German-born French engraver, illustrator and painter.

A WEDDING

Page 159 — **Adolphe Houdard and Pierre Veber**: Houdard was a writer on political, social and economic subjects. For Veber, see note on *The Soldier's Hat*.

— ***La Revue bleue***: *La Revue politique et littéraire*, a political magazine published between 1871 and 1939.

— **my youngest brother**: Colette had three siblings, a half-sister and half-brother from her mother Sido's first marriage: Juliette, born 1860; Achille, born 1863, and a full brother: Léopold, born 1866.

Page 160 — **Vigée-Lebrun**: Elisabeth Vigée-Lebrun (1755-1842). A society portrait painter. Marie-Antoinette was at one time her patron. She married at twenty, like Colette, and is said to have had doubts even on her wedding day. Her husband proved to be a spendthrift and womaniser.

— ***"Mauri, tu ris, tes saluts tentent"***: the literal meaning is Mauri (Maurice), you laugh, your greetings are tempting. When spoken, the line is a punning version of Morituri te salutant (We who are about to die salute you).

Page 161 — ***De jucher les champs sur la mine***: Achille's mini fable says:

A mine-works gapes, a field just above it
Slips, and suddenly disappears with a loud crash.
MORAL
Beware, for as long as you live,
Of placing your fields above a mine.

The moral comes from the last two lines of a fable by *La Fontaine*, Book 6, No. IV: *Le cochet, le chat et le souriceau* (The young cockerel, the cat and the young mouse), in which the young mouse, frightened by the flapping wings and bright colours of the cockerel but reassured by the smooth and silent cat, is warned:

Garde-toi, tant que tu vivras,
De juger les gens sur la mine.
(Beware, for as long as you live,
Of judging people by their looks.)

— **...old man Hugo**: Victor Hugo (1802-1885). Poet and dramatist, grand old man of 19th century French literature. His poem, well-known to all French schoolchildren, comes from the collection *Les Feuilles d'automne* (1831) and begins:

Lorsque l'enfant paraît, le cercle de famille
Applaudit à grands cris...

— **Baudelaire**: Charles Baudelaire (1821-67). Poet, author of *Les Fleurs du mal*. These are the first two lines of his poem *Recueillement* (Meditation).

Be still, my pain, and calm yourself with peace.
You called the evening down; it falls; it comes.

The next two lines, which the Colette figure will have had in mind, continue:

A darkening atmosphere enfolds the town,
To some souls bringing rest, to others grief.

The second line is in fact a minor misquotation, Colette having *Tu demandais…* where Baudelaire has *Tu réclamais…*

Note how Colette, the author, invents these word games, all of which suggest dire consequences for the new status of 'Colette', the character.

Page 162 — **Sully Prudhomme**: René François Armand Prudhomme (1839-1907). A poet and essayist, he was the first winner of the Nobel Prize in Literature, in 1901. His early works were sentimental, his later ones largely philosophical.

Page 166 — **Beatrice Cenci**: (1577-1599) was a Roman noblewoman imprisoned by her father, who repeatedly raped her. She killed him to escape his abuse and was beheaded for her crime, despite outpourings of protest. See Shelley's play *The Cenci: A Tragedy in Five Acts* (1820).

— **Barberini Palace**: Il Palazzo Barberini is a seventeenth century palace in Rome, housing the *Galleria Nazionale d'Arte Antica*, the main national collection of older paintings in Rome. Caravaggio's *Judith Beheading Holofernes* is in the Palazzo Barberini—said to be modelled on the beheading of Beatrice Cenci, which Caravaggio witnessed.

Page 167 — **Sadi Carnot**: (1837-1894) became President of the Third Republic in 1887. He was assassinated in 1894. He wore a thick black beard and a heavy moustache.